A NOVEL BY

irene schram

SIMON AND SCHUSTER · NEW YORK

ashes,
ashes,
we
all
fall
down

Win

First printing

SBN 671–21212–5
Library of Congress Catalog Card Number: 72–75049
Designed by Edith Fowler
Manufactured in the United States of America
by H. Wolff Book Mfg. Co., Inc.

All the events and characters in this book are fictional, and any resemblance to persons living or dead is wholly coincidental.

for d. a. levy

GOD'S LOVE

The soft young man named Jonathan, with a
pink face, yellow-blond hair, and a lisping voice,
ran home and put on priest's clothes, even though
he wasn't a priest. But he wanted to be. He came
back in a black dress with buttons all the way
down the front, and a white lace collar, and walked
around for us. We are two cats—all black, with
white yokes, white lace throats. He is our father.

"Do you love God?" he asked us.

We turned and walked away. We walked all
around the room like priests too. He took this for
"no."

"But it doesn't matter," he said. "God's love
is irresistible. If you don't love him in this world,
you'll love him in the next."

But we don't.

—FOLK FABLE

Ring Around a Rosie

Ring around a rosie,
A pocket full of posies,
Ashes, ashes,
We all fall down.

—Nursery Rhyme

Our whole class of students was on the grass, in the park, for a picnic: it was April and time for a picnic after a long winter full of weeks and months of rain, boring rain. Of course there was the snow too, and no one minded that, but there wasn't that much of it and it kept being washed away by the rain, all winter long, while we were kept inside for months and months, until now, waiting for spring. But now at last it was spring again and we were outside again, and we'd come to the park for a picnic.

And we weren't doing anything wrong. The grass had just come up a few days ago, so it was still green and sweet and soft, and the fence around it had just been opened up so people could go in and sit on the grass, for the first time in the spring. But you were supposed to be careful not to hurt it. The grass, I mean. When we first got there we all ran onto it and flopped down, and some of us laid our faces in it, because it felt and smelled so good, but we weren't doing anything wrong. Though it was true that as soon as our bodies were in the grass we got a little silly, because it was so beautiful, and some of us rolled on it or did somersaults and cartwheels (Jeffrey stood on his head, no one else could) and some, our teacher saw, just couldn't keep from lacing our fingers in and out of the beautiful new green stalks, no matter how hard we tried, because it felt so good to do it that our fingers nearly did it by themselves in the first place. They laced themselves into the grass, and almost started, the way you do, grabbing hold of single pieces or whole handfuls of it to pull up, wanting to hear the little-sweet sound there would be as the grass broke off at the bottom or popped out of the earth at its roots.

But we *didn't*. I already said we didn't do anything wrong. What happened was this: Miss Love saw our fingers as they began lacing into it, and stood up and got all our attention, and asked us not to hurt the grass because we had so little of it. But she smiled too, and said it meant a lot to her that we didn't, even though she knew how hard it was not to and how good it felt to do it. So we all stopped. But our hands kept going back to the grass again and almost doing it, we couldn't help it. It was a kind of loving, and we'd catch ourselves just in time to stop, over and over. Then Miss Love saw and stood up again and said she could see we were still having trouble, and someone, Yvette I think, said just what I was thinking, "It's not that we *want* to, Miss Love, our hands just keep on going back down there all by themselves!"

"I know," Miss Love answered, "it is hard. But I think I know something that will help you. It is just another thing you can do with the grass that also feels very good on your fingers. Watch me and you will see."

So we all watched to see what she would do. Miss Love is the best teacher any of us ever had, and we all try to do what she says. Love is a good name for her, just as it's a good word all by itself: love. Miss Love is Oriental, from a place in Japan, and her real name is a word no one can say. But she told us "love" was part of its meaning in English, and that's what we could call her. She's beautiful and very tiny, just like a doll, some of us are as big as she is. And she's very gentle, and never yells, and has such a beautiful quiet voice. My voice is pretty quiet too, but it isn't beautiful the way Miss Love's is, you just can't hear it sometimes. Miss Love's voice is gentle and soft, but you can always hear what it says, and it sounds like music because it's so sweet and goes up and down a lot in the middle of sentences, and says each syllable strongly, like my name, Nadia, Miss Love says Nad-i-ya, instead of Nad-ya like everyone else. I like it. It sounds much prettier that way.

But everything Miss Love does is pretty. In school she gets us to be quiet and pay attention just by standing in front of the room and smiling, without a sound, until we see her waiting there and one by one stop making the noise. Then she smiles an even bigger smile at us and says, "Thank you," and her voice makes us feel so good we're not sorry at all we had to stop. She has shining black hair and eyes, pink cheeks, and tan skin.

She said, "Watch me, watch what I do," and got down on the grass again but with her knees tucked underneath her, leaned forward, and spread her hands out flat, with her fingers stretched as far apart as she could get them, so they curved up a little at the tips. She put her hands down on the ground just that way, so many pieces of beautiful green grass bristled up in between her fingers, and turned her face up to the sun. Then she tipped her head as far back as she could, until her face was almost flat and parallel with the blue sky—and then, with her eyes closed, she held her hands stiff and started moving them, slowly, up and down in the grass, and the grass *moved in return*, in and out, in and out of her fingers, the green blades disappearing and then appearing again and stroking her hand. While the sun washed her face.

"Now it is your turn, children," she told us when she stopped. "You try it."

It felt wonderful. Except that it was even better, it was the same feeling you get at night, when you lie in your bed, your head comfortable on the soft pillow, and let your hair run long and cool in between your fingers. It's a good way to go to sleep. And the grass-stroking felt just like it, but better because Miss Love and all the other children were doing it too, with the sun flooding and washing all their faces, and the greenness of the grass and the way it was growing out of the brown, happy, warm, alive, earth.

It was wonderful, and kept our hands safe from pulling up the grass, so it worked.

We all did it for a while. No, wait: only some of us did, though no one pulled up the grass. But some children were eating lunch already, and some were too happy and excited just to be there to do anything quiet. Some of the boys and some girls too, like Jackie Becker, who's a tomboy, and Lizabeth and Aliysha, two of the kissing girls, who like to chase boys and kiss them, were running around and tagging each other. Jeffrey did some flips, and then stood on his head again.

But a man saw him and came over saying, "That's very good!" He watched for a minute, and then said, "Come on, straighten up your legs some more." Jeffrey's face got very dark and red. From standing on his head, but also from being angry, you could tell. Jeffrey has dark skin, but it gets even darker and deep red when he's angry or embarrassed. It's from all the blood racing underneath.

The man was strange, and Jeffrey didn't like him standing there telling him what to do. His clothes were dirty and his hair was wild and frizzy and much too long around his face, so it was really like girls' hair. "Look, like this," he said, and Jeffrey flipped down and watched him hop over upside down onto *his* head, and get his legs and his body perfectly straight up into the air, with his baggy pants sliding down around his knees. I remember, he had on black tie shoes and no socks. But suddenly he threw his legs back down, jumped onto his feet, reached out and grabbed Jeffrey and picked him right up off the ground. Jeffrey's tough, but it was very scary, and Miss Love and all of us who saw started to be afraid, but then the man looked over at us, especially at Miss Love, and put Jeffrey right back down. Then he said, "Hey, do you know how to play ring-a-levio? I bet you can run fast, can't you!" And he crouched down and got ready to leap and run and Jeffrey ran away.

Some of the other kids joined in then, Paul and Jackie and Peter. But the man only wanted to catch Jeffrey. And he couldn't: Jeffrey's the fastest runner in our class, and he was much too fast for the man. So it just went on that way for a while, with the man trying to catch Jeffrey and Jeffrey running first one way and then another, then stopping and starting over, and both of them red in the face and sweating. Then I stopped watching for a while, since it wasn't scary anymore and I was hungry and un-wrapping my lunch, and the next time I looked Jeffrey was back with us and the man was gone, all the way over at the other corner of the grass, by himself. Jeffrey sat down and put his face in the grass, and Miss Love smiled at him.

"Yes, you can also lay your heads down in the grass," Miss Love said, smiling at Jeffrey, "and it will be cool

and fresh and tickle your noses and you will all smell it."
So some of us did that too.

And we never did anything bad.

But from that moment on bad things began to happen
to us, and they haven't stopped yet. That's why I'm writing this. I'm going to write everything down in this book,
and then we'll try to get it out of here to find us help. But
I can't do any jumping ahead. I have to tell it all in exactly the order it happened, because Miss Love says that
is the best way.

We live in The City, our school is in The City, and it
was a City park we were in that day. That's why the grass
was so precious. I'm sure there must be some places, like
in the country, where you don't have to be so careful
with it. Once we all had to write things about where we'd
like to be, and I wrote this poem about it:

> *In the Country*
> by Nadia Johnson
>
> Someplace there are colors
> I can see.
> Blue and purple,
> Green and yellow,
> Someplace the grass is,
> It is lovely to walk around.

The grass is a hint: all the colors are the things you see
in the country. Blue for sky, purple for flowers, yellow for

the sun and green for grass. In The City there are less colors, and a lot is gray. For example our school is pretty close to the park, but the park isn't pretty, it's just three or four blocks of dirt, with a sidewalk around it and benches along the sidewalk where people can sit. But then, all around the sidewalks, so of course around the whole park too, is The City. Buildings. No, wait. First the streets: avenues on two of the sides, regular streets on the other two, and fast traffic driving by all the time. Cars and trucks, buses and taxis, police cars and motorcycles and fire engines.

And then, across the streets, come the buildings. Office buildings and big apartment buildings, all very high. And they're very old buildings too, sooty and dirty and old, and they all have old incinerators, so everything else is dirty all the time too. Everything, even the grass. The shoots of grass that come up green and beautiful every spring get covered with soot before they're a week old. But most of the time we ignore the soot, we don't even notice it. Like the way we leave our houses every morning for school, scrubbed and clean, but get there with gray hands and faces and clothes instead, and don't even notice it enough to wash it off.

But I think about it. Like at the picnic, I mean, I knew, really all of us knew, that a week from that day it wouldn't even be nice enough any more to sit in the grass, and we'd have to be crazy to put our faces down on it! We could do that once or twice every spring, if we got there right after they took the fences down, but that was all. After that the grass began dying, from soot, and garbage, and just too many feet walking over it all the time, it would die, and the ground itself, the spaces of earth in between all the blades of grass that grew bigger each day, soon wouldn't even be earth anymore, it would be garbage-patch. Because plastered all over it would be dog mess, cigarette butts and matches, broken bottles, paper, soda-can rings, ice-cream sticks and even those little rubber bags that are for sex—we know all about it. And that's just to name some.

But we're used to it, and to the streets with trucks and motorcycles roaring along them all the time, and people you have to walk around in a big circle, and big buildings everywhere, that you live in, and that have incinerators in them that burn up some of the garbage and send the rest of it floating down in ashes onto you and the grass and everything else. And right then, as we sat on the new grass together, from over the top of one of the buildings terrible, filthy dirty incinerator smoke started pouring in even worse billows than usual into the air. It was really thick and black, and by the time it reached the ground the air had changed it only a little bit toward gray.

Soon the whole sky over the park was turning gray. It must have been more than one incinerator at once, because there was dirt all over: big flakes of soot, ashes blowing everywhere, and even unburned pieces of garbage, smoky edges of papers and food and thrown-out things that the flames somehow hadn't quite burned up. They were floating all around us, and many of us, looking up without thinking first, got things in our eyes and couldn't see. It was so thick our noses and throats hurt.

And then it started being hard to breathe, and Miss Love said we had to go.

We hadn't really had our picnic lunches yet, and now the whole day was spoiled. We all complained, "Oh no, it isn't fair, can't we do something about it, Miss Love?" We knew we couldn't stay where we were, but we didn't want our day to be ruined either. But Miss Love said there wasn't anything we could do about it in time to save our picnic, though as soon as we got back to school we were all going to write letters of complaint to the Mayor and the Air Pollution Board, and maybe something could be done soon so this would never happen again, to us or anyone else.

"But if only there was somewhere around here where we could eat, away from the smoke," Anthony said. "It could even be indoors, but just not back in school, so we could still have our picnic."

Miss Love was shaking her head, sure there wasn't anyplace we could go, when Mark suddenly shouted, "Look! What's that over there!"

"Where could it have come from!" Lexi cried, jumping up and down with excitement.

We couldn't believe it. We couldn't remember ever seeing it before, but now there was a little house right at the edge of the grass across the park. "It must be a brand-new shelter they have built," Miss Love said. "We will go and see." So holding each other's hands in the grayness, we went over to the house.

The door was open, and we peered in. It was pretty

dark inside, because there weren't any windows, but we could see it was cheerful enough. At least it was a lot nicer than it was outside. There were little tables with chairs around them, enough for all of us, and a row of soda and candy machines against the wall. "Come, children," Miss Love said, "I am sure it will be all right to go in." And we all went in the house.

The minute we were inside the door clicked shut behind us, locked, and we were prisoners.

And somehow we knew it right away, even though nothing else happened for a long time. They didn't come for us until later. But as soon as the door shut behind us all by itself and we heard the click of the lock, we knew something was really wrong, more than just the wind blowing the door shut or some other kind of accident like that. And we also realized that we should have known, and never gone in at all, because how could something just appear like that out of nowhere? Because then we were sure it had never been there before.

And when we stopped staring at the door and turning the knob and trying to open it, and turned around and looked at the room again, we saw that all the tables and chairs and food machines had disappeared—or else had never been there in the first place! Both of those things were impossible, but one of them had to be. Because they were really gone. Everything was, and it was very dark, much darker than when we first came in. But that was only because of the door shutting, and there being no windows. We could still see, just, because a little light crept in through the wooden boards that made the walls of the house, but it was very dark.

Miss Love was so upset she didn't look like a grownup at all anymore, she looked like a child of our own age, ten or eleven. She kept looking around and saying, "I do not understand this. Imaginary things cannot become *real*, real things cannot disappear." Behind her, the kissing girls were holding hands and crying. The three kissing girls are Aliysha, Lizabeth and Donna. Or they used to be kissing girls before we got here, because back at school they spent almost every recess chasing boys and catching them and kissing them. They'd pick out the boy they wanted and just keep chasing him until they caught him, and then two of them would hold him down on the ground while the third one kissed him.

But now they were not kissing, they were crying and holding hands and hiding behind Miss Love, and many other children were too, boys as well as girls, like Mark and Steven and Paul. It had suddenly gotten much colder in the little house, and with everything gone, the tables and chairs and candy machines and everything, and how dark it was too, it was really a bad place to be in. And then, after a long time, the door opened again, and they were there.

Many men with bad, mean faces stood in the doorway. They had real guns in their hands, and they didn't say a word. Miss Love said, "Leave us alone, who are you, let us go," but they never opened their mouths or made a single sound with their voices. They captured us and put us in big black cars and took us here, to this place where we've been ever since.

Wait, first I have to tell about the cars.

They were so big and long and black that they frightened us almost as much as the men did, and Miss Love was very upset about us having to get in them. But she told us to try and stay calm, and do exactly what they wanted us to do, and that included getting in the cars. She said we were much less likely to get hurt if we did what they wanted. "Do not be afraid, children, you must try hard not to be afraid," she said to us. But the cars were frightening, and we were afraid, and even she was, even Miss Love. Then after they started going Paul said, "Miss Love, these are *hearses*."

I was in the same car as Paul and Steven and Miss Love. They just shoved us all in the cars, four or five of us in each, and I was lucky to be with Miss Love.

"What's hearses?" said Steven.

"Hearses," Paul said again. "*Dead*-cars. Cars they put the dead bodies in, when somebody dies."

So Steven giggled at that. He always giggles, all the time, and he giggles the hardest when he's scared of something. I gasped at it, and even Miss Love looked shocked. But when I asked her if it was true, if it could be true, she said yes, they could be hearses.

And I'm pretty sure they were. They were completely black, inside and out. Even the bumpers and door handles, which should have been silver, were black, because everything was. The tires were of course, and the steering wheel and seats and rugs and roof were black too. All black. The men were wearing black uniforms and black helmets, and the air inside the car was so dark and heavy we could hardly breathe it in and out, though it still wasn't as bad as the pollution outside.

Even the window glass was black. There was a little slit in front of the driver so he could see out and not crash, but we couldn't tell a thing about where we were going. I started to cry. I couldn't help it, and then I heard Paul crying too—I didn't see him because I had my hands over my face, but in between my own crying I heard him crying too, and Steven still sort of giggling, but his giggling sounded almost worse, sadder, than our crying. Sometimes we felt like we were on a kind of terrible merry-go-round, the way the black car kept sailing smoothly like a boat around and around corners, very gently and gradually, with the turning seeming to go on forever. But at last it ended, and the car came to a stop.

The Man with the Gun

There was a little man,
And he had a little gun,
And his bullets were made of
    lead, lead, lead.
He went to the brook,
And he shot a little duck,
Right through the middle of the
    head, head, head.

              —NURSERY SONG

There's a spiral staircase in the hotel, leading from the lobby up to the rooms we sleep in. It's made of black metal, and has no guardrails or bannisters, even though it's so steep and high and winds in such a tight spiral that it's dangerous to walk on. And we have to walk up it to get to our rooms. The minute we saw it, before we'd ever been on it, we were afraid of that staircase, it just looked so dangerous all by itself—and that was before we had any idea that they wanted to kill us, and had to make us do it to ourselves. But as soon as we'd been on it once, and that was right away, we understood, and then we were really afraid.

We had just arrived, and were standing all together in the hotel lobby, frightened but a lot better than we would have been without Miss Love. As soon as we were out of the cars and inside the door, the men who brought us disappeared, and we were left alone—but only for a second, because suddenly many other men with guns rushed in and made a circle around us.

Miss Love looked at them, and then she told us to stay where we were and walked right up to one of them and said, "Please, tell me who you are and why we are here." But he didn't answer her. He didn't even look at her, so she asked him again and when he still didn't say anything she went to another one and asked him, but he didn't answer either. She reached out and touched his arm, to make sure he knew she was there, though of course he did, but he still didn't answer. And she tried another and another one, and they never moved.

But she didn't let them know she was upset, and just turned around and came back to us. And then we stood there, waiting and not knowing what would happen. No one said anything, and we were so scared of them not moving and not saying anything that we didn't even cry, we were silent too. We stood as close to Miss Love as we could get, and she tried to hold all of us at once, but we were silent, with all our screaming going on inside us, only looking at each other and never at their terrible

30

faces. And then they pulled their triggers and shot off their guns!

Our ears hurt so terribly we couldn't believe it. We were holding our heads and screaming, and running everywhere to try to get away, not caring how, pushing and shoving each other. It was so terrible, because they didn't stop, they kept shooting their guns, and each time was worse than the one before. But then somehow Miss Love got us to listen to her, and in between the shots she told us they were only shooting blanks, making a lot of noise but not firing any bullets, so they couldn't hurt us. And then she said this: we were not to do anything else they said, because they were bad, evil men. We were to help each other, and *resist*.

That was the first time the idea came up, the word and the idea of resisting. It's been with us ever since. In every way, all the time, we must resist. We must all stick together and help each other, stay in our group and never separate, and refuse to do what they want. And we must try not to be afraid.

We did try, but we were still afraid. And we tried not to do what they wanted, but we had to, because the next thing we knew, with the terrible sound of their stamping, stamping feet, but not a single word ever, they came straight at us and started pushing us and slapping us hard, and they never said a thing. We all moved. With Miss Love in the middle, we moved just the way they wanted us to, in a screaming mob up the black spiral stairs.

31

It was such a long, terrible way up. The stairs had no bannisters at all, nothing to grab for balance, and they twisted so narrowly around and around, that children kept being pushed to the edge and almost falling off.

And then we started to understand that they wanted to kill us.

Somebody looked down over the side of the black spiral staircase and caught his breath in horror, and then one by one the rest of us saw, and we all gasped. I wish we had never looked. It was so terrible I felt my knees slip and I almost fell. They were pushing and hitting us to make us move up the staircase as fast as we could so we'd be sure to fall, and it was so steep that anyone who did fall would certainly be killed just crashing on the floor below, but even so they must have thought that wasn't enough, because what we saw when we looked was them, down there, scattering sharp, broken glass all over the floor underneath, so that anyone who fell would be cut to bits. Some of the men were doing that, and the rest were still behind us, keeping us moving in a mob so we'd never get in any order or line at all, but instead push each other off the stairs, or lose our balance and fall off by ourselves!

And Miss Love, in the middle of such terrible danger, Miss Love was smiling, just managing to smile, while she kept saying, "That is right, children, help your classmates, try and help one another. We must slow down, and everyone is to help each other, that is right."

And little by little, terribly slowly, we did it, we made ourselves slow down. The children at the back had the worst time, because the guards were still behind them, pushing them and hitting them and never stopping. The back children had to take it. But they were so brave and did, Jackie and Susanna and Paul, and our class got hold of itself at last, and slowed down and held onto each other so no one fell off those terrible stairs. No one, even though we were all crying so hard, all of us except Miss Love. I don't know how she did it, but she did: she kept smiling, small-smiling to help us, and it saved us all.

So they never succeeded at that trick. They tried it again and again, but every time Miss Love managed to smile and that reminded the rest of us to hold onto each other and help someone, and no one ever fell off. Oh, and it was always when we were going up that it happened. They never bothered us on the way down.

And we were a group. From then on, even in this terrible place, even they could see that none of us would ever do one thing to hurt any other one no matter what, and we'd always try to help each other instead. Miss Love says that is a wonderful achievement and we should all be proud of ourselves, and we are.

But I don't think I told enough about the guards yet. I didn't really tell much about them at all. I told how they wear all black, but that's all. Well, the worst thing about them isn't the black, it's the way they're just like machines. They're all dressed the same, in their black, and it's so black you can't see anything but its blackness. You can't see any buttons or wrinkles or what kind of cloth the uniforms are made out of, and in the dark you can't see them at all. They even wear black gloves. So there are only their white faces showing, and those are white, white, white, as white as the black is black. They all look the same, you can't tell them apart. And they never move their faces, to smile or frown or scream or threaten you, and if you say anything to them, the way Miss Love tried to in the beginning, they act as though you weren't even there. When you get hurt they don't look glad, because they don't look anything. Never, because they never move their faces and they never make a sound, not counting with their bodies. They move their bodies all the time, they stamp their feet and smack with their hands, and turn their heads to look at each other and maybe speak to each other that way, silently, but they move their faces never. Ever.

That's what the guards are like.

Then one time they had us at the bottom of the stairs, but things were different. We could tell right away. The guards were there all right, but we knew something was different, somehow, and then we started up the stairs, and there was no shooting over our heads and no rushing at us to make us run. We couldn't believe it, but we kept going, walking, slowly, our backs sucking in and expecting it to begin any minute—and it didn't. So then we started to relax and smile, just a little, like Miss Love, thinking could it be true that we were beginning to beat them? And if we were, what would happen then? Would they send us *home*? If they saw we weren't going to give in, ever, but were going to stick together and not hurt each other and always look out for each other instead, and resist and resist, would they give up on us and send us *home?*

There are a lot of steps on the spiral staircase. I never counted them, but there are a lot, probably forty or fifty, and every one of them twists. And when we started to relax we were almost all still at the bottom of the staircase, and some of us hadn't even started up it yet. Miss Love was somewhere in the middle of us. She always walks in the middle, so she can reach and help the most children at once. She had one arm around Steven, and the other around Mark, the biggest child in the class and also the most frightened. Mark is much bigger than anyone else in our class, even Miss Love. And he's not skinny, he's a little heavy. But he acts younger, not older, than the rest of us. He cries the easiest and acts the worst. Steven's terrible too, but he just gets paralyzed when he's scared, and giggles until he can't even move and we have to help him and drag him, but when Mark is afraid, which of course is almost all the time around here, he instantly falls down on his hands and knees and turns around and tries to crawl away from the danger as fast as he can, and of course it looks ridiculous, because he's so big, and should be helping Miss Love, and should be encouraging us all, and he isn't, and because he's so soft and sort of jiggles as he crawls away. He looks ridiculous. And it's part of *resisting* that we all look proud and serious, so Miss Love is working hard on him so he won't let all the rest of us down.

So Miss Love was in the middle helping Steven and Mark. Greg and Donna were in the front of the class, just because that's where they happened to be, and we were all moving together the same as always. But then Greg reached a certain step on the black spiral staircase, put his foot on it, and the step shot out to the side! It shot right out of the line of stairs all the way to the side, with Greg on it, and tried to throw him off. But somehow he stayed on, and just as suddenly and quickly it shot itself back into place, so hard it knocked him into all the children behind him. Half of us swayed backwards and almost fell.

It was a new trick the guards had. Suddenly they were all behind us again, not letting us stop, and many steps on the stairway were moving. Children were putting their feet on them and being shot out screaming to the side. Everyone was crying, and even Miss Love couldn't smile anymore.

We tried to freeze on the stairs and not move, but the guards kept pushing us so hard that we couldn't stop even though we knew the steps would keep shooting us out. Steven stepped down on one of them and Miss Love grabbed him just in time, and then all at once Donna was pointing and screaming, "This one, this one!" Somehow she spotted one before she stepped on it, and stopped herself and screamed and pointed at it so we all missed it. Tears were streaming from our eyes and our stomachs hurt from fear. Then Miss Love spotted another one, and I don't know how but she figured it out, and suddenly she was crying, "Children, count the stairs, it is every seventh one! Step over them, count!" and we began to. Mark started crawling, and Miss Love pulled him back up on his feet, saying, "That will not help you, Mark, you must step over them . . . now! That one!"

And we managed to spot almost every seventh step. Crying as we went, we climbed up the rest of the way by stepping over every one we could, and made it to the top with only a few more children getting on the wrong ones and being shot out sideways, but always with the hands of their classmates reaching out and grabbing them and holding onto them until the steps smashed back in. And no one fell off. The guards' fury rumbled and thundered in the air all around us, but as soon as the steps got back in, with the scared-to-death children still hanging onto them, hands pulled them off and the climb went on, until at last we were all safe at the top and stumbling together into one of our rooms, where we fell on the floor panting and crying. Miss Love waited to come in until every one of us was in first, and then she came in and just stood there looking around at all of us, exhausted, her face wet with crying and trying to control herself. Finally she said, "I am proud of you all," and a minute later, "Is everyone all right? Is anyone badly hurt?"

Steven giggled.

Miss Love looked at him and said, "Yes, go ahead, Steven, please laugh now. Everyone, laugh if you can. Laughter will help us so."

But of course no one did. "No," said Miss Love, "of

course not. You cannot laugh just because someone tells you to, can you." And she sat down next to Steven to rest.

"And anyway, we can't laugh because nothing's funny around here," Anthony said.

"I want to go home," Karen said, starting to cry again.

"Yes, Miss Love, we don't understand anything around here!" Greg cried. "Where are we, why do we have to be here? Can't you tell us? Why *can't* we go home?"

"And Miss Love," I said, "how can steps just move like that!"

"That is a very good question, Nadia, and Gregory, yours are too," Miss Love said. "But I am afraid I cannot answer them. You know I would tell you the answers if I knew them. But I promise I will try again to find out, and as soon as I discover anything at all I will tell you."

And that was all. And Miss Love still doesn't know. Even she doesn't.

And this is where we are now: a big, open space, made of just dirt like an empty lot, but big enough so we haven't seen all of it yet, even though we've been here long enough. But almost everywhere you look there's just dirt, and then a high metal fence around all of it, the same kind they have around schoolyards, made of wires that cross over each other to make diamond-shapes—but much higher than usual. And the fence tilts inward at the top, and instead of the wires being turned down to make it safe the way they're supposed to be, they're left sticking straight up, as sharp as knives. But they won't hurt us, because we've tried climbing the fence when the guards weren't around, and we can't get to the top. We start off fine, but it's just so high, and as we go up it gets harder and harder. The metal is rough and hurts our fingers, and our toes hurt too, because only the tips of them can fit in the holes. But the fence keeps going and going. If we look up we see we still have so far to go, and we can't, and if we look down it's much worse, because we really are high up already and it's so far down we get dizzy. And then we always go back down. Our fingers ache and ache, and sometimes our feet miss a hole, they think they're in one but they're not, and we start to slip and almost fall. Even the kids who are usually good at climbing can't. And one day Miss Love tried, she tried so hard, but she couldn't either.

Only one of us might be able to do it: Jeffrey. He climbed very far up it, and could have gone on and on until he reached the top, where it tilts, and then held on very tightly and tried to lift his legs high up past the points, to get over it and down the other side. But instead he climbed back down, and now he's sure he can do it but he's trying to teach the rest of us how so we can all escape. And that's strange, because he's usually a *terrible* boy. He's our class problem and troublemaker, and steals things and bullies everyone, and Miss Love had to tell him two or three times already that if he didn't improve he might have to be transferred, maybe even into Mrs. Santana's class next door, and everybody hates her. And now he's being so good, a good friend and helper to us all, trying to teach us how to climb the fence so we can escape. "Just hold on and keep going, keep going and don't look," he calls after us while we climb and climb, "don't stop and don't look down!" But only part way up we have to stop and climb back. We just can't do it.

So we're still here, and inside the fence there's just one building, the hotel. One big hotel, that we all have to stay in, and not just our class either, because sometimes we see other children too, though we're never with them and don't know who they are. And even the guards. They're separate from us but in the same building. But now at last it is time to really write it in this notebook— it's been so hard waiting—the thing that is screaming around in our minds every minute, every second in this terrible place, but I couldn't say it until now because Miss Love told me to be sure to tell everything in order. But now it is time and I can say it: they are keeping us here and they are trying to *kill* us!

We're sure of it. Even Miss Love had to admit it at last, because we all knew it, and her pretending it wasn't true wasn't doing anybody any good. We know it, it's been proven. They're trying to kill us, and we've even seen a graveyard, with lines of little mounds of the graves of dead children. The only reason we're still alive right now is that they can't do it just by murdering us. Even Miss Love doesn't understand it, but we've figured out that they have rules here, and have to follow them, and the rules say they may not murder us but have to trick us, fool us, or in any other way they can, make us die all by ourselves. And we must resist and try *not* to be killed.

We've seen some older children here too, thirteen or fourteen years old, and a couple of them even older than that, almost as big as the guards. Almost grown up I mean. But they're really all alone. We never see them talking to each other, and we're not allowed to talk to them. We are not allowed to talk to anyone not in our own class, they hurt us if we try. But what we think is the older ones were captured children just like us, who have been here for a long, long time. They must have come with their classes long ago, but not stuck together, the way we do, and some of them escaped, some been *killed*, and a couple of them are left over now, with no group and no one they can be with or talk to. They look so lonely, and they're still here after so long, it could be years and years if they came when they were the same age as we are now, and still, all they can do, every minute of every day, is try to keep from being killed. Because if they stop resisting they'll die, there are traps everywhere! Of course they must know all the old ones by now, but I bet the guards keep coming up with new ones! It's terrible. At least we have each other. And Miss Love!

I am the best and fastest writer in our class, and Miss Love gave me this job to do: writing a record of everything that's happened to us, in this notebook, which is the only paper we have because Miss Love had it with her when we were captured, and then keeping it up to date. Miss Love can't write it herself because she's too busy, every single minute, taking care of us. So I'm doing it instead. My name is Nadia Johnson and I'm eleven years old. I'm going to be a writer when I grow up.

We sleep in little rooms. There are beds and then a kind of dry toilet thing in the corner that you have to use, without a door around it or anything so you always have to tell everybody to look away, and then there's another room with showers in it that the guards took us to. We had to take showers in it together, more than one at the same time, but luckily it only held about six or seven of us at once, so Miss Love could separate the girls and the boys. But then we went in and got undressed and washed ourselves with soap, and washed our clothes too, and squeezed them out and put them right back on, wet, because no one has any extra ones. And we had to be very careful while we were in the shower, because all of a sudden the water would get hot enough to burn us before we had a chance to jump out from underneath it. Then we'd have to wait until it was cool enough to go back under again and finish washing. That happened two or three times before we were finished, and we were lucky that no one got hurt. But I guess they'll take us there once in a while, and that's the only time we'll get to wash at all, as long as we're here, so we'll have to do it and just be very careful each time.

There are four beds in each little room, all big and soft, with mattresses and pillows and cushions and covers all over them, but we don't sleep in them. We discovered the first night we were here that they were dangerous: they collapsed, burying us under piles of smothering covers. So we sleep on the floor instead. Miss Love says it is the only way. She says if we ever once give in to the softness, we will be in trouble. We have to keep on resisting.

So we sleep on the floor all night, three of us at a time. There are four of us in each room but one has to stay awake, on guard, because we have to have guards too. It's very hard to be the one on guard. You have nightmares when you're sleeping, but on guard at night you're afraid of everything. You sit in the corner behind the door, where a little light comes in from the hall, with your back against the wall so nothing can come up behind you, and you're so scared that you press too hard against the wall and soon your back hurts, but if you don't do it you're more scared than ever, and you can't really decide which is worse, to be so scared or to hurt so much. Usually you'd rather hurt. And then your neck hurts too, because you can't stop turning your head all the way around to the sides, one side and then the other and then back again, so you can see all the places in the room that you think you hear strange noises coming from, where things might be hiding.

Miss Love knows it scares us, but she says we have to do it, for safety. But she comes in to talk to us as often as she can, and she always comes when it's time to wake up the next one on guard, to talk to them and try to get them more cheerful about it before they start. And then they do start, and you're finished guarding and can go to sleep. Miss Love almost never sleeps, but she has to soon. She looks so tired it's terrible. I'm on guard right now, in my room, waiting for Miss Love. I keep writing because I'm less scared when I do, so I just don't stop writing or let my mind hold still even for a second, when I'm on guard, because I can't stand it if I do. I just keep thinking things and writing them down. I think of home and my mother and my room and other things too, like the housing hotels, I keep remembering them because they're a little like here. Many children in our school come from them, though not anybody in our class. But some children have to live in the hotels because their parents don't have any money, so they have to have welfare, and welfare won't pay for their apartments any more or else their buildings burn down, and then they have to live in hotels because there aren't any empty apartments left in our City.

But the hotels are terrible. Of course they're not as bad as here, because they're not really prisons the way this is and no one's trying to kill the children there. But they have rats, which we don't, and sometimes the children in them have to sleep in rooms far away from their mothers, and their fathers aren't even there anymore. And they have accidents all the time in the hotels, so maybe it is as bad as here. And they get killed too! They get killed on stairways when the stairways cave in, and the elevators, some children in a housing hotel died in an elevator accident just before we came here, and one of them was a girl the same age as us, and we knew her. I just keep thinking about it—we didn't get killed on this stairway here, but they wanted us to, and we almost did. And other things, like the way we have to be separated from Miss Love sometimes, because she just can't be in every room at the same time, and we're not always all in the same room, like at night, when we sleep, and sometimes we don't see her for so long. And Miss Love's just like our mother, here. So maybe this is almost like a housing hotel.

And also, we're all so hungry. We don't get enough food to eat, just a tiny bit. So we're very hungry, and the kids who live in housing hotels are always hungry too.

There are twenty of us here. Eleven girls and eight boys, and Miss Love. And Miss Love had her pocketbook with her in the park when we were captured, so we have her comb and mirror and even her little nail file. We clean our nails and comb our hair every day—and Donna combs her hair in the morning and the night, and Gail combs hers all the time, because she loves it and can't stand it to be tangled. But anyway we can't wash every day because all we have is a little drinking water, and we can't afford to wash with any of that. So I guess we'll only be able to wash when they take us to those showers.

We sleep in five different rooms, and I'm on guard in mine. All the kissing girls are sleeping. They're all in my room, Lizabeth and Aliysha and Donna. Aliysha's having a dream, and she's moaning and moving all around in her sleep. I wanted to be in the same room with Joanne, because we're best friends, but Miss Love asked me if I would please stay with the three kissing girls instead, and then Joanne would be with Karen and Susanna and Gail, because Miss Love thinks we can help take care of the others a little bit because we're more responsible. Then Miss Love's in the room with Jackie, Yvette and Lexi, or that's where she's supposed to be, to sleep, except she almost never does, she just keeps moving around from room to room all night. And with the boys, Anthony's in charge of one room and Paul the other, but I don't know why Miss Love picked Paul, I think Greg would be better.

Donna will have to wake up soon, because she's on guard next. Miss Love will be here in a minute to wake her up.

How long can Miss Love keep going without really sleeping though? I don't know.

Miss Love says before I go any further, and catch up with the present and start writing everything down just as it happens, I should put more information in here about all of us. Names, and everything.

We are class 5–502, which is a fifth-grade class in P. S. 75, 4th Avenue and 7th Street in The City. Miss Love is our teacher, of course, Miss H. Love. That isn't her real name, but even the principal uses that name for her. And there are 22 children in our class, but only 19 are here, because three were absent the day of the picnic. We only have 22 children in our class because we're a special class. We know it. We're very smart, we're the best class in the school. Everyone says so, even the principal, Mr. Gaffney. We've given two plays in the auditorium, and our class has more things in the school paper every month than any other class. Stories, and poems like the one I wrote about the country, that was in the paper. Anyway, the children in our class who are here are (girls first):

Nadia Johnson
Susanna Todd
Karen Elvers
Yvette Duval
Joanne Novo
Alexis Hill (Lexi)
Aliysha Elkind
Lizabeth Rich
Donna Joffey
Gail Skelly
Jackie Becker
Mark Toberman
Gregory Lyons
Steven Black
Anthony Maris
Jeffrey Davies
Kenneth Ling
Peter Borreca
Paul Weaver

Eleven girls and eight boys. Valerie DeBrosca, John Russell, and Patrick Robinson are the ones who were absent the day of the picnic. Back in school, I don't know what they did with them. I guess they're in some other class now.

I'm sitting in our room right now. It's about the only place around here that's kind of safe. Well, not really safe, but pretty safe. They don't let us stay here very much, though. But right now we're all here, and I'm sitting against the wall behind the door. The guards keep passing by along the hallway, and I don't want them to

see me writing here, and this way if I hear someone coming I just lean over to the side and hide behind the door.
I can even see out a little, through the crack where the
door attaches to the wall, so I know when it's safe to sit
up straight again.

The thing I just don't understand though is how we're
all getting so used to being here. Because in between the
terrible things that keep happening to us all the time we
just seem to keep going along from part to part of our
days, every day, talking or even smiling or laughing sometimes, when you'd think we'd be frightened and crying
all the time. It's bad enough here for that. But Miss Love
won't let us, and besides, which is what I just said, we're
getting used to it a lot now. Maybe it's because of growing up in the middle of so much wrong with the world,
the way I said we were used to the pollution and the incinerators and everything, because they've always been
there, or the way we know there's a war going on, but
we're not scared, because there's always been a war going
on and it doesn't scare you anymore when you're so used
to it. And we sure are, we've been seeing the pictures and
hearing the body-counts on TV since we were two years
old.

And we know about the other troubles in the world
too, everything I guess, since they happen every day. We
know all about the world ending soon, if people don't
stop dirtying it up all the time with every single thing
they can think of, like paper, tissues and toilet paper, the
way you shouldn't use the colored kind because the dye
from it gets into the water, the ocean I guess, after you

flush, and just never gets out, and the fish get poisoned from it and then you eat the fish. And drunks, and drugs —we know about everything. So maybe another bad thing, this I mean, just isn't that much of a surprise to us. It's happening to us now instead of everything else, that's all.

I remember once in school, a long time ago but I can tell it now because Miss Love said to put in a lot about us, and it's about us, when Miss Love started talking about cannibals. She said they could still be found in some faraway places, and started to tell about them. But Miss Love always says she learns a lot from us, just the way we learn from her, and here's what she means: when she was talking about cannibals that day, Anthony raised his hand, and when she called on him he said, "Miss Love, last night on the news I saw a naked girl with a cut right down the middle of her belly."

"Oh, Anthony, you are telling us stories," Miss Love said.

"No he isn't, Miss Love, I saw it too," Kenneth said. "It was a picture from the war."

"All right, I see. And you would rather talk about what you saw on television than about the cannibals I read of?"

We were all sitting in the back of the room, on our chairs, which we'd brought back there and put around in a circle for discussion. We have discussion every morning in school, when Miss Love sits on a child's chair just like the rest of us, and as soon as we're all settled she says, "Who has something to speak about today?" Or sometimes she starts the discussion herself, the way she did that day when she said she just read an interesting article about real cannibals, and wanted to tell us about them. "You mean you do not want to hear about the cannibals?" she asked us. "I am so surprised."

"Yes we do, Miss Love," Mark said, "but first what about that girl's cut? I didn't see that, what was it about?"

"Well then, Anthony will lead the discussion, as I did not see it either," Miss Love said.

So Anthony started telling about it. But about half of us saw it on TV too, on the six o'clock news, and children kept interrupting him while he was talking. Then he got very upset, because he hates to be interrupted. Anthony has light blond hair, little eyes that are blue or sometimes green, and a very pale white bony face. And when he gets mad, his skin just gets whiter and paler until you can almost see his veins through it, but his eyes get red and the tips of his bones, like his cheekbones and nose, burn like fire. That happened then. But Miss Love saw, and said, "No, children, let Anthony tell about it first. He is the one who is telling it. Afterwards you will all have your chance to add things, or to ask questions. Anthony, please go ahead."

"It happened in the war," he started again. "American soldiers went pretty far to get to a place where there were supposed to be a lot of enemy soldiers hiding. But when they got there it turned out there weren't any, there were only a lot of women, mostly old, and children and old men. But the soldiers were so angry at coming all the way there for nothing that they killed them anyway, even though they weren't the enemy, because they couldn't be because none of them were soldiers. How could they be, they were all too young or too old. But they killed them anyway. They burned all the houses up and shot the people and stabbed them and stabbed them with knives. It took a long time because there were so many, hundreds of people I think the news said. Babies too—and kids, boys and girls."

Steven started giggling and didn't stop.

"This is not a thing to giggle at, Steven," Miss Love said to him.

"There must have been a lot of blood and stuff," said Greg.

"It happened a long time ago, about five years ago. But it was only on TV last night. The girl wanted to get even with the soldiers for killing her mother and father and brothers and sisters and everybody else she knew too, so she finally got the idea of letting them take movies of her for the news with her clothes almost all off, so she could show the scar. She got it from American soldiers, and now everybody's angry at them. And she escaped because they thought she was dead. But she wasn't, she was bleeding and bleeding, but she was one of the last ones they killed because they raped her first, even though she was only *eleven* years old then. And then they left fast, so they'd be gone before anyone came and found out about it, and somehow she got the blood to stop running out so fast, and then someone came and found her and took her to the hospital and now she's all right. Except she has the scar, and she doesn't know anybody, because everybody she knows is dead."

He stopped talking for a minute, but nobody said anything.

"It was such a terrible scar, too," he went on, "so ugly. She wasn't all the way naked, but she was on the top, and she had her skirt pulled all the way down past her belly. It went right down the whole middle of her body, Miss Love, from her neck to where she still had her skirt on, but pulled down, and it still didn't end there, but you couldn't see it anymore. And you couldn't see her belly button! It was gone, sucked right into that scar that was so red it looked like a false color on the TV. We get them sometimes. But my father said it was the scar that was all red like that, not the TV."

"What else did your father say, Anthony?" Miss Love asked him.

"He said it was too bad and I should change the channel," Anthony said. "But I didn't. I wanted to look at that scar. You know, it probably almost cut her in half, except then it didn't."

"Yes, Anthony. It is very sad," said Miss Love.

"Do you think it hurt her an awful lot?" Donna whispered.

"Oh yes," Susanna answered, "it must have."

"Yes," said Miss Love, "I am sure it hurt terribly. I am sure it was more pain than any of us has ever felt."

"A million times more," Greg said.

"And I think this too, children, how sad it is that you must know of such terrible things when you are so young.

But there is something still sadder: that such things have to happen at all. I certainly do not want to speak of cannibals now. We have talked enough for one discussion period." Then she stood up and picked up her chair to carry it back to where it belonged in the room, and the rest of us got up too.

"But Miss Love?" Anthony said.

"Yes, Anthony?"

"I wanted to say the body-count for yesterday. I thought I should tell it. It was 42 American, 16 Allied, and 427 Enemy."

But most of us already knew that.

Jeffrey tried to climb over the fence today, and it was a trap. You can't get over it. He almost died!

And he wasn't going to leave yet, either: the guards weren't around and Miss Love just wanted him to try it, to see if he could do it, and then he was coming back, and tomorrow or the day after he was going to leave. That was the plan Miss Love thought of, since no one else can climb the fence, for him to take this book, after I wrote all the information in it like our names and school and how they captured us and are trying to kill us and everything else, and try to get over the fence with it, and when he found someone to tell, give them the book so they would believe him. He didn't want to go without us, but he finally said he would, and he was just trying it, to see if it would work.

He started climbing, just the same as the other day, but this time he didn't stop but kept on going, so high, all the way up, very, very slowly. Finally he reached the top. He got himself steady and reached his hand out to grab the top of the fence for balance so he could step over the sharp pointed ends of the wires without getting hurt.

It was electric! The minute he touched the top there was loud buzzing and a terrible flash of light that seemed to come right out of his hand. And a smell, a sizzling smell, his hand burning!

He would have been killed, but he wasn't because luckily he touched the top of the fence so carefully that it didn't give him a big enough shock to kill him. But it hurt him a lot, and he lost his balance and fell. He came plunging back down, and I don't know how high that fence is but it's higher than a house! We were all bunched around the bottom when it happened, watching him, and he landed on us. So we broke his fall, and he wasn't killed, and now nothing seems to be broken. One of his ankles is swollen all up and he limps and aches all over, and he's covered with bruises, but we think that's all. But many of us were hurt, because of his body landing right on top of us, and Lexi's nose may be broken. She cries all the time, and looks so frightened, because it hurts her so much. And there's nothing Miss Love can do about it, because there's no one here to help us. She just keeps telling Lexi it will heal, and she's staying close to her all the time because it hurts her so much.

Now we know why they don't watch us closer when we're near the fence.

And now we know we can't get Jeffrey out with the book to get us help, so I don't know what we'll do.

Something terrible happened.

I was on guard, writing about Jeffrey and waiting for Miss Love to come, when suddenly I heard something loud outside our room, coming up the stairs. I didn't know what it could be and jumped back behind the door, very frightened, and then I heard a boy's voice and all at once Anthony fell into the room. I thought he'd just had a bad dream, but then I remembered I heard him coming up the stairs, and I saw how he looked. He was crying and shaking all over, and holding a blanket wrapped around him, and his hair and face were soaking wet. He made so much noise that everyone woke up. Miss Love came running in a second after him, and everybody else ran in after her.

"Anthony, what is it?" she said, rushing over to him.

"No, don't touch me!" he screamed, clutching the blanket tighter around him.

"Anthony, what on earth is the matter? Is something underneath your blanket? Why are you holding it like that? You must take it off and show me!"

"I can't, I can't!"

"But what happened! You must tell me!"

"Oh please, Miss Love, I will, but don't touch me, please don't let anybody touch me! You can't see yet!"

We were all staring at him and feeling so frightened, waiting to hear what it could be. He was holding the blanket so tightly around him, and we didn't know why, but we knew it was going to be something terrible.

"All right, Anthony," Miss Love said. "No one will touch you, I promise. But you must tell me quickly what happened to you."

And so, very quietly, and shaking so hard that sometimes we could hardly understand him, he started to tell us.

"I was asleep, Miss Love, and I had a horrible nightmare. I was in a desert, but it was black, it was a *black* desert! And first I thought I was dead. The sand was so black, and so hot it burned me, I could feel it burning and burning. Everything was so hot, and my hands and knees and legs were burning up because I was *crawling*, I couldn't walk! My legs couldn't walk, but the sand was burning me and I couldn't stand still so I had to crawl. And I couldn't even breathe anymore, the air was so hot it hurt me to breathe, and it was so horrible, because I *had* to keep breathing or I'd suffocate! But every time I took a breath my throat and my tongue hurt so much. And then I woke up, and it really started, Miss Love, what really happened just started *then*.

"I was in my room. All the others were asleep. Kenneth was on guard, but even he was asleep. And we were all lying on the floor, but the floor was burning hot! Just like in my dream, but real! I knew I should wake up the others to tell them, because I was burning up and I thought they must be too, and just not know it, and I should tell them, but I didn't because the floor was so hot I couldn't stand it and had to run. That's why I had that dream, Miss Love, because the floor was *really* hot. And then I started acting crazy. I got up off the burning floor and I decided to go outside."

"Oh, Anthony, by yourself?" Miss Love said. "You know you cannot do that, it is too dangerous!"

"I know, but I did, I said I didn't know what I was doing, Miss Love, I . . ." He stopped, and looked the other way.

"All right, Anthony, it will be all right. Go on now."

"I was just acting crazy, Miss Love. I wanted to go look for you, but I kept thinking I wouldn't be able to find you even if I looked and looked. So I got up and went out of the room, and then I got the idea in my head about going outside, and I went down the stairs! They were so hot underneath my feet I couldn't stand it, and I almost ran down, except I was too afraid to. But nothing happened, on the stairs I mean, there was nobody around, no guards and no one. I thought that was funny, and then I just thought I was lucky. And I went *outside*."

He had to stop talking for a minute again, he was shaking so hard. Miss Love put her arm around him to try to comfort him, patting his shoulder where her hand reached around, and this time he let her touch him. "But are you all right, Anthony, are you not hurt?"

Then suddenly she caught her breath and cried, "Anthony, what is that blood?"

We all looked where she was looking: at the very bottom of the blanket wrapped around Anthony, where red was beginning to seep out onto the floor.

"Anthony, what is it!" Miss Love cried, her face white.

"You must take off that blanket, you are badly hurt!"

"No, don't!" he screamed.

"But, Anthony, what happened to you!"

"I'll tell you, Miss Love, only please don't take off the blanket yet, don't, please!"

"All right," she said finally, "I will wait until you are finished. Continue and finish as quickly as you can!"

Then he started talking faster. "I was so burning, burning hot when I went out the door, and so thirsty I couldn't stand it. Thirsty all over, not just for a drink, my whole body burning. I started running. First I went straight, and then I don't know why but I turned around and ran back behind the hotel instead. The fence is much further away in the back than in the front, and I went on and on, running and running but not getting anywhere, and my body was still hurting and hot and burning! And then I saw the pool."

"The what?" Susanna said. "A swimming pool? There couldn't be a swimming pool here!"

"No, not a swimming pool, a pool of water, right here, somewhere in the back! Like a pond, I mean. I was running and suddenly I saw it and stopped. I don't know, it wasn't very big, and it didn't look dangerous. I was so hot, and the water just looked cool, and I wanted to swim in it."

"But do you know how to swim?" Paul asked him.

"Of course he does," Donna said. "You got your beginner's, right, Anthony?"

"No, my intermediate! That's why I thought I could just jump in the pool and swim until I cooled off and it would be all right. Anyway, I *had* to, if I didn't get cool fast I was going to burst into flames and burn to ashes. So I walked the rest of the way to the pool, to jump in."

He stopped talking.

"And then?" said Miss Love, her arm tightly around him. We could see a lot of blood by then. More and more of it was coming out from underneath the blanket, because the blanket wasn't soaking up any more. So much!

"And then I walked onto it, and it was ice."

"Ice? Anthony, it is warm out, it is the springtime!"

"I *know*. But it was crazy like everything else, Miss Love! Everything was crazy. It looked like water, and I was burning up, and it's warm out, but it was ice. It looked like water but I walked onto it, and it was so *cold* it burned the bottoms of my feet as badly as the black sand in the desert did."

"In your dream?" Karen asked him.

"Yes, in my dream, in my real dream. I mean my dream that was so real I woke up really burning, and had to go out. It's like everything was dreaming, except it was real. I was awake." He started shaking hard again.

"It burned my feet, and I fell down. And suddenly the ice cracked, all at once, and I fell into freezing black water!"

Anthony was crying now as he talked. "I just sank under. It was too cold to swim, nobody could have, but when I came back up I was still burning! Even in that freezing cold water. I was burning *cold*. Then I did try to swim, and I could move in the water, but big pieces of ice were floating all around me, and I couldn't really swim. I tried to climb out of the water onto the ice, since big parts of the pond were still all ice and I thought of that, but I couldn't, and the ice cut me, it cut my hands, see?" He pulled his hands out from under the blanket one at a time to show them to Miss Love, and then jerked them back under again. They were bleeding from cuts and scratches all over them.

"I thought I was going to drown. And then all at once the ice started melting! It went so fast I could see the pieces getting smaller while I looked at them, they just kept melting and melting and getting smaller and smaller, until they were all gone! All the ice was gone, there was no more. I even wondered if I'd just imagined it, maybe it was never really there at all. Then I started swimming to the edge, to get out.

"But I couldn't get there. I just kept swimming around and around in circles. And then I saw the fish."

"Fish? Were there fish in the pond, Anthony?" Miss Love asked him.

"Yes. Little fish, swimming all around, around and around, just like me. I thought maybe they were caught in a whirlpool that was making them go round and round like that, and I was too. I didn't want them to touch me, but they were just little fish and I wasn't afraid of them. And then I saw their teeth."

"Teeth! Fish don't have teeth, Anthony," Steven said.

"Yes they do," Anthony whispered. "Piranha do."

"Piranha!" Greg cried.

Anthony was shaking so terribly we could hardly hear

him. "They chased me around and around. Then they reached me. They started to bite me."

"Anthony!" said Miss Love.

"They bit my leg."

"Your leg, Anthony!"

"No, they didn't get my leg, I swam and swam."

"Your foot!" Greg screamed.

"No, not my foot. I swam so fast, I screamed Help, Help, but of course no one came. Then I got to the edge and climbed out. Blood came out of my foot and my, my toe . . ."

Miss Love reached for the blanket, but he was still holding it on tight. "I started to run. It hurts so much, Miss Love, and I ran and ran. I got back in the door. I came up the stairs and somebody helped me, gave me the blanket and wrapped me up. I counted steps, I didn't step on any seventh, Miss Love—"

At last he let her take the blanket off him.

His clothes were soaking wet, and he was freezing. His right foot was covered with blood, and his big toe was gone.

Of course there's no doctor here. We don't know what we'll do if anyone gets sick and needs medicine or anything like that. And Miss Love didn't know what to do for Anthony.

As soon as she pulled the blanket off him we could see how terrible it was. Blood was pouring out of his foot where his toe had been, but wasn't anymore, because it was gone. There was nothing there but ragged skin and blood and dirt, and we had no water to wash it with. But Miss Love said the first thing was to stop the blood. "Bring a sheet from one of the beds, someone, as fast as you can!"

Donna ran and got it, and then Miss Love tried to rip it to make a bandage, but she couldn't. It just wouldn't rip. She tried with her teeth, and she still couldn't, and all the time Anthony's foot went on bleeding, and he was moaning and keeping his head turned away from his foot because he didn't want to see it. And Miss Love was just bunching the whole sheet up to get it around his foot any way at all when a voice we didn't know whispered, "Here, use this," and we all looked up.

There was a stranger in the room with us.

I remembered Anthony said someone helped him up the stairs and gave him the blanket, and I thought right away this must be him. He was very tall, and looked about eighteen years old. But he was so long and thin he seemed more like a kind of animal, maybe a cat or a fox, than a person. He was just so skinny, and he stood very strangely and moved quiet as a cat. And he had dark skin and green eyes and a beautiful mouth with wide, curved lips. He was a prisoner just like us. But he was one of those older children who must have been here for a long time, and even older than the rest of them. He really wasn't a child anymore, he was a man.

He stooped down next to Miss Love and gave her a big handkerchief, and Miss Love wrapped it into a bandage around Anthony's foot. Then he stood up again.

"Wait, I'll be right back," he said, and he left.

We all sat there, and no one said anything. There was so much to say but no one began. Anthony was still sitting up, and moaning and moaning, with his eyes shut and his head turned away.

And then he came back and somehow he'd gotten two more cloths, one wet and one dry. He gave the wet one to Miss Love first, and she peeled the old bandage off Anthony's foot. It was soaked with his blood. As gently as she could, she took the wet handkerchief and wiped off most of the dirt. Anthony never moved. It must have hurt him a lot, but he just kept moaning the same as before. Maybe his foot was so cold he couldn't even feel it. Miss Love kept saying his skin was like ice. She finished and wrapped the dry handkerchief around his foot, and bunched the sheet around that.

"Now put him down flat, with his foot highest," the stranger whispered to Miss Love. "Wait, let me do it." He took Anthony and gently lowered him back, and down, until he was flat on the floor, and then Miss Love got another sheet and he bunched it up and put Anthony's foot on top of it. But he shook his head. "It's still not high enough. It should be higher than this," he said, and he got two blankets and put them under Anthony's foot too. Then Anthony opened his eyes for a second and said, "He's the one who helped me."

Miss Love got a pillow to put under his head and another blanket to cover him with.

"He'll probably be all right now," the stranger said, smiling just a little at Miss Love. "I saw him struggling up the stairs like that and I ran and got the blanket to wrap around him. And I wanted to carry him, first I wrapped the blanket around him and then I tried to pick him up. But he wouldn't let me."

"You have helped us so much, I do not know how to thank you," Miss Love said, and then he really smiled. "We will never be able to thank you enough. But please, you must go before you are caught. You must not be hurt because of us."

"Oh, I'm not worried about them," he said. "They won't catch me. I've been here so long, I know what to do. And anyway I don't care if they do catch me."

"But what would they do to you if they did?" Greg said to him.

"Oh, maybe kill me," he laughed. "A little. More."

Miss Love reached out and touched his arm, but she jumped back in surprise. "Oh! Your skin, it is hot!"

"Oh, don't worry about that, it always is," he said. "I'm used to it. I have a fever, that's all. I always do, I've had one all my life. A hundred and two or a hundred and three. It's just the way I am." He smiled at her again. "When did you get here?" he said.

"Well, perhaps several days ago," Miss Love said. "But how long have you been here?"

"Oh, perhaps several years!" He started to laugh, but he stopped right away. "Look, if you just got here, you must all be pretty hungry. But just don't worry about it, they'll give you more food soon. They always practically starve you first, to see what that does, but then they start giving you enough. Hey, wait a minute." Then he reached into his pocket and pulled some bread out of it!

"Want this? It's not enough for all of you, though."

We all stared at the bread in his hand.

We're so hungry. We still only get a little food every day, little bits we find in our rooms, that Miss Love shares out, probably just enough to keep us from really starving. So we stared at the bread. Mark started to whimper, and Steven started giggling. Miss Love looked at them and then away again without saying anything. And my mouth was wide open, and I was holding my breath.

"That is very kind of you," Miss Love said, "but . . ."

"Wait, I have . . . I'll be right back," he said, and slipped out the door.

This time he was gone longer. Miss Love tried to smile at us.

"Do you think he'll come back, Miss Love?" I asked her.

"Is Anthony going to be all right, Miss Love?" Kenneth said. We both talked at exactly the same time.

"Oh yes, I hope so," Miss Love answered. "He said he would come back, and I am sure Anthony will be all right."

And then he came back, and I don't know how he got it but he had enough bread for all of us! "Here," he said, "I think there's enough for half a slice each."

Miss Love reached out and took it, and then very quickly gave us each our piece. But she took a whole slice for Anthony. "He must begin to regain his strength," she said. Anthony opened his eyes and saw Miss Love holding the bread, and let her put it into his hand, but he didn't open his mouth. "Please, Anthony, you must eat it," she said to him, "you must get better, and it will help you, please." Finally he opened his mouth and started to eat the bread.

It was the middle of the night. Miss Love looked around at us. We had all finished our bread. "You are exhausted, children, you must get some more sleep now," she said. "Go back to your rooms please, and try to sleep a little more before it is morning. I am sure Anthony will be all right, and we will talk tomorrow. Goodnight."

We didn't want to go. We hate to be alone, which is what being away from Miss Love always feels like, even if we're with other children. But we did what she said, because we always do.

Most of the kids in our class are ordinary, but I'm supposed to tell about them anyway. I'll just tell a little.

I already told about Mark. He's very big, but babyish. He acts younger than almost anyone else, only Steven acts younger than him. Steven is short and fat and very silly, but he's silly all the time, and sometimes Mark isn't.

Donna, Lizabeth and Aliysha are the ones we call the kissing girls. Miss Love says they act too old, and I know Donna does. She's very pretty, with long, pale blond hair and tan skin, and beautiful blue eyes. Oh, and she's very small. I mean there are other girls in our class as small as she is, like Aliysha, and Yvette's even smaller, she's the smallest of all, but Donna's funny about it. She likes boys, and likes being small so she can stand up very close to them and have to bend her head all the way back and look up to see them. Anthony is supposed to be her boyfriend, but she really flirts with all the boys. And Lizabeth and Aliysha are a lot like her, just from following her around all the time. They like boys too much too. Aliysha has brown hair in a ponytail and blue eyes and a turned-up nose. Lizabeth has brown hair too, but curly and short, and brown eyes.

I am very bright. I could be in the sixth or seventh grade, Miss Love says so, but I'm only old enough for fifth, even though I'm eleven now. But I don't care because I love Miss Love and I'd hate any other class, and anyway Miss Love always lets me help her with the real hard work, like writing this. I am tall and have brown eyes and dark brown hair. Lexi, Alexis Hill, is the next tallest girl after me. She was always so funny, except she isn't anymore. But she used to be, before we came here and before she hurt her nose, she was just like a clown. She's tall and skinny and has very short pixie-cut black hair and can do things with her face, and she always moved fast and jerkily. She used to be so funny. But we were always laughing *with* her, and not *at* her. We laugh *at* Mark and Steven sometimes because they're so babyish. It's especially hard not to laugh at Mark, because he looks so big, but acts so little.

Jackie Becker is a tomboy, but nice, but ugly. She never wears dresses. But she's best friends with Yvette, which is very funny, because Yvette's just the opposite, small and girlish and quiet and always in dresses. And

Yvette's mother and father are French, and don't speak English. Susanna's black, with Afro hair, and she's beautiful. She's the next tallest girl after Lexi, and they're friends. Kenneth Ling is Chinese and very well-behaved. He never gets in trouble in class and has his homework done every single day. Greg says Kenneth's father beats him with a strap if he does anything wrong in school or if he doesn't know how to do the homework.

Jeffrey is a bully and has been caught stealing things, but sometimes he seems to get a little better, and here, I said already, he's being very good. Paul is strange. Sometimes he's a sissy, but he tells a lot of dirty jokes. And a man lives in his house that his mother's not married to, but he bosses Paul around just the same. And Paul's mother and the man hit Paul too, like Kenneth's father hits him. Sometimes they even hit Paul in the face. In the beginning of school he had a black eye, and he said his mother did it, and he used to say his mother was a witch, but he doesn't anymore. Miss Love helped him. She helps everybody. She just loved him a lot and when he got to love her back she taught him not to say things like that about his mother. I bet that's what happened.

Anthony is serious all the time, and can't stand being teased. Miss Love says what she wants most of all is to teach him to laugh. Oh, and he loves Donna. A lot of the kids have girlfriends and boyfriends. Not me, but Donna and Anthony, Greg and Joanne, Peter and Lizabeth, and Kenneth and Gail.

Karen and Gail are best friends, and so are Joanne and

I. Karen's blond. I don't like her very much, and she hates me. Gail's okay—she has very long hair. Straight and brown, and she always wears it down and combs it a lot. Joanne is the best reader in the class. She's very serious too, just like Anthony, she could be his sister. They even look a little alike, with the same kind of pale skin and bony faces, and they both hate to be teased. She loves Greg though. I like him too, but he likes Joanne. And Peter is short and smart, and that's everybody but Greg.

He's very nice. Susanna calls him beautiful Gregory (and he calls her ugly old Susanna). He's very good-looking, tall and strong with sandy brown hair and big blue eyes. He draws beautiful pictures, and we found out here that he has a lot of nightmares. The boys in his room with him complained that he was waking them up every night shouting and screaming. But Miss Love told them we all dream a lot and she's heard every one of us crying in our sleep since we came.

It's true. Last night I dreamed I had to climb a fence to get out of a churchyard I was in. I was locked in and couldn't get out. Well, I climbed up to the top of the fence all right but then I was afraid to jump and couldn't get down. Miss Love was standing right there, but *outside*, and she wanted to catch me or lift me down, but I cried, "No, you can't, I weigh too much, no one can lift me, you don't know how much I weigh." She kept saying she could do it, but I never let her. And I never got off the fence.

But Greg dreams the most. He told us what he dreams

about, Miss Love asked him. He dreams about giant things most of the time, giant ants and spiders and snakes. But he says since we got here he keeps dreaming one thing over and over. He dreams that our whole class of students is on the grass again, just the way everything started, and we're holding hands in a big circle and singing songs. We're very happy. But the grass isn't our park, it's a green field somewhere, he doesn't know where, but it's big and wide and couldn't be the park. Then suddenly, from far across the sky, heading straight for us, comes a whole flight of giant black butterflies, that Miss Love said stand for the pollution that really came down. Thousands of black butterflies flutter and fly into the air of the dream, darkening it and darkening the whole sky. And as they come some black music grows in the sky too, but somehow it's backwards, and very deep and slow, with drumbeats and crying horns. Greg was still scared about it while he was telling it, and we were too, and no one laughed. The music grows and grows until it hurts our ears, and all the butterflies flutter around the children's heads, around our heads, over the green grass, and then come down to land, and when they do they become nuns, in black gowns and hoods, who raise their black gowns and hoods into the sky over our heads and then bring them back down on top of us, smothering us so we can't breathe, and Greg wakes up screaming, That's the dream.

They leave us alone a lot here now, the guards I mean, and sometimes we start thinking we're safe, even if we're so far from home and don't know where we are. And now at last they're giving us more food too, we find horrible packages of crackers or bread or old fruit or bottles of juice in our rooms every day, and enough for all of us now, so we're not worried about starving anymore. Even though the food doesn't taste good and it's never enough to fill us, it's still food and we're not going to starve. So sometimes we start to think we're safe and we'll be all right. But we never think so for long before something happens, the old things like the stairs or else new things, new traps.

But so far we're still all right. Anthony's foot is a little better, I guess. He limps terribly but he can't get his shoe on now, and he moans because it hurts him so much but he can just about walk when he has to. We haven't seen the place where it happened to him though, the pool, because we're all afraid to go and look. And besides, the morning after what happened to him, as soon as we woke up, Miss Love talked to us for a long time about all of us trying not to let anything like that ever happen again. She said we mustn't ever go outside by ourselves, and especially to keep away from the back, and we all have partners now, with the three kissing girls together so it comes out even, and we can't do anything alone except keep guard. And then Miss Love said this: that she was sure Anthony would never, never have done that on his own, so we all must, we had to, from then on, stop and stop and stop and think about what we're going to do, before we do it, every single time, because she thinks they may have ways of telling us right inside of our minds

what to do. And what they tell us will always be something that's bad for us, and good for them.

"But do not be frightened, children," she said, "I do
not mean it is any kind of magic, there are ways to do
those things. So do not be afraid, but be sure you are
always very, very careful."

Miss Love just came and gave me this to copy in here.
It's a list on a little piece of paper:

DUTY REGULATIONS

PROHIBITED ON DUTY OR
WHEN ANY PRISONERS PRESENT:
    Bodily Functions
    Speech or Facial Expression
    Communication with Other Guards
    (Except Eye-Signals)

PROHIBITED AT ALL TIMES:
    Willful Murder of Prisoners
    Assistance of Injured Prisoners
    Communication with or
    Response to Prisoners

Prohibited means forbidden.

Miss Love said she got it from the man who helped
Anthony, and his name is Raymond. I asked her where
he found it, and if he knows where this place is, since he's
been here so long and must know so much, and he can
talk to us. But she said he doesn't know anything, the

same as us. He just found the list and gave it to her.

And when she gave it to me Miss Love also said that pretty soon she was going to tell some of the other children they could write in here too. We've been having trouble lately with some children crying a lot with unhappiness. They wish they could be home, and they're so scared here. They want to be where someone else will take care of them again, like their mothers and fathers. Miss Love does things for everyone, but there's only one of her and so many of us that we have to take care of ourselves most of the time. But she thinks letting all the children who want to write in this book too will help, because they'll feel busy and important doing it, and it will also help let off some of their unhappiness.

It's night again, and I'm on guard again. I always write when I'm on guard.

But Miss Love must have told the others right away, because she just gave me the list and told me about the others being allowed to write in here soon, and then left, and I just had time to finish writing about it and then stopped and was thinking, and now Mark is here and says he can write in the book too. So I am giving it to him now.

My name is Mark Toberman. I am ten years old. I live at 242 1st Avenue. My phone number is 555–6702. My father's name is Mark too. My mother's name is Alice. I have no brothers or sisters.

They captured us and now we're all prisoners. In the

war. But we don't have to fight, we're only prisoners. We will never see our homes again. Miss Love didn't tell us that, but I know.

I keep thinking I'm dreaming and then I don't wake up. We just live here and they try to kill us and that's all. They are just waiting for us to get killed and die, and we're trying not to. But I know they'll win.

MARK

Now he gave it back to me. But I can't write any more because my guard time is over and I have to go to sleep.

An even more terrible thing happened now.

It was the middle of the night when it started. The children on guard started screaming, and then everyone else woke up screaming too, because suddenly the lights were flashing on and off and the walls shuddering and terrible sounds and shrieks were coming from somewhere down the hall. We were all standing around in huddles in our own rooms, too scared to look for Miss Love or get together. And then Miss Love came and got us all into one room, but the screams and noises were shuddering all around us, and Miss Love kept saying, "Stay right here! Everyone! We will not move!" But the noise just grew louder and louder and the lights flashing on and off and on and off made us grab each other so no one would slide off or get sucked away somehow, because it felt like that could happen. And then Miss Love was crying, "No! Stop!" at Jeffrey, who was moving and heading for the door of the room.

But he wasn't walking. He was *leaning*, bending toward the noise. "Jeffrey, come back!" Miss Love cried, but he didn't, and soon we all knew he didn't because he couldn't, because all at once all our bodies were leaning and pressing us over to the door and out of the room too. The shrieking and shuddering and flashing was pulling us to itself like a magnet, and Miss Love moved too. I think she could have resisted it and not moved, except she had to, to come with us.

So we all moved slowly out the door of the room. Our feet and legs felt like they were walking in glue, they could hardly pick themselves up and step and step. But they couldn't *stop* moving either, even though they tried to, we tried, Miss Love tried. "No, children, stop!" she cried. "We can't, help us!" we screamed back. And we kept moving, around the corner of the doorway and into the hall and down it.

Soon we were further down the hall than we'd ever gone before. It was much longer than we'd thought. It went on and on, passing doors to start with but then becoming just a terrible, empty hallway with nothing in it but the screams and noise and walls shuddering and shaking, and then it started getting wider. Wider and wider, as we kept moving down it, and the terrible noises all around us got worse than ever, until they hurt, so much, and they grew and grew with every second, hammering inside our ears—until finally, suddenly, it was over.

There was no more noise. It just stopped. Then the walls stopped shaking too, and finally the lights stopped flashing on and off, but stopped with them on, glaring and bright. And we stopped. It was completely still, and we stared in front of us and couldn't believe it: there, at the end of the noise, in the wide and glaring end of the long hall, were cars!

Cars. Not toys but real ones, big and long and black. About ten of them, yes, ten, because then we all got into them, and two were in each and everybody was in. And it must have been just like what happened to Anthony because no one said anything or decided to do it, but we all got into the cars, just like that. Two in every car, the driver and one other, both in the front. There was a back seat too but you couldn't get into it, because there was no back door and the top of the front seat almost touched the roof.

We didn't plan who would go in together, we just got in. I didn't know where Miss Love was, and I know I didn't think it was a good thing to be getting in the cars, or that we were going home or anything. Nobody thought that, because nobody thought anything. We just got in, and closed the doors, and the cars started to go! The ones sitting by the steering wheels put their hands on them, but didn't press the gas or start the motors, and the cars started. All we could do was hang on and try to steer, while the roaring of the cars filled the whole hallway like a hurricane, with all the cars racing so fast, and their motors and tires screaming. And they were all facing in different directions when they started.

I was sure we were going to crash. But we didn't right away, because the children in the drivers' seats managed to turn their wheels just in time, and all the cars missed each other and kept going. And the only good thing happened then: the minute we turned the wheels to try to save ourselves, we got ourselves back. All of us, not just the ones turning the wheels. After that they weren't in control of us anymore, and we could at least try to resist again.

But even though we didn't crash and we were back in control of ourselves, we still weren't saved. The cars kept going, and very soon they were far enough down the hallway so they reached the part where it started getting narrow again, it did in both directions. In another second there were going to be too many cars for the space of the hallway to hold, and we'd all smash against each other and be killed.

We searched for the brake pedals and found them and stamped on them, and we stopped in time. But the engines were roaring with power and bursting to go again, we couldn't hold them back! We were standing on the brakes, pushing them down with our whole bodies as hard as we could, but they were getting away anyway, they were too strong for us. And then they did. They exploded forward with a huge jerk and knocked us back into our seats again, panting and crying, while they started racing down the hall again. I was the driver in one of them, with Gail next to me, and we were just about to crash into the side of the next car when I heard Miss Love's voice shouting near us:

"Make it go backwards! Push the stick on the wheel to the place called reverse!"

"Where is it?" I screamed, and others screamed, looking for it, but our hands were shaking so hard that we couldn't find it.

"*Reverse! On the wheel!*" Miss Love screamed as loud as she could.

"On the wheel!" I heard Anthony scream after her from far down the other end of the hall, where all the cars were now that had been aimed in that direction. He'd heard her and was trying to let the other cars down there know what to do too. "Push it to reverse to go backwards!" he screamed. Then we found the R for Reverse and pulled the sticks there, and the cars shot backwards, safely away from the narrow ends of the hall where they would have crashed against each other—but at a terrible speed again, horribly fast, all towards the middle. And we couldn't slow them down a bit, even though we stood on the brakes trying to.

We crashed in the middle of the room.

Everyone was crying, and many children were hurt. At least the cars were stopped, all locked together in a huge pile in the middle of the room, and kept by all the cars around them from moving again. But cries and screams were coming from everywhere. Then Miss Love's voice came again.

"Who is hurt! Who is hurt! Children, climb out as quickly as you can! Call if you are badly hurt and I will come and help you!" At least then I knew she was all right.

Children began answering her right away. "I can't get

out!" "I'm stuck, help me!" "Miss Love, help, I'm bleed-ing!"

"Everyone, help! Please children, move! Help who-ever you can," Miss Love cried.

"Miss Love!" It was Kenneth, who was still inside his car like most of us, and his voice was full of terror. "Miss Love, the motors are still running! We'll all be poisoned! Look at the air!"

It was turning black. The cars weren't moving any-more, but their motors were still going and pumping black smoke and fumes into the air of the room. "We have to get out of here or we'll all be poisoned!"

"Quickly, children, quickly!" Miss Love was climbing over cars to reach us and get us out. "Move, children, even if you are hurt! Get out right now, the air will be poisoned soon! Please help me, children, climb out, do not be frightened!" But a lot of us felt so scared and sick we weren't moving, we were still sitting in the cars, and every minute the air was turning darker with filthy stink-ing gas fumes that turned your stomach. Then at last we started to move, and in the darkness of the fumes every-one began to struggle out of the cars, coughing and crying.

"Try not to open your mouths, children, breathe as lit-tle as you can," Miss Love said, and then choked on the smoke herself.

Almost everyone was hurt, a little or a lot. You couldn't tell how badly right away, but all of our faces were bleeding, and some children couldn't get out of the cars. Miss Love pulled at the doors to try to open them, and two of the boys who were hurt the least did too, Paul and Greg. When Miss Love couldn't get doors open she took her shoe in her hand and broke windows with the heel, with the children inside those cars turned away and crouching against the seats so they wouldn't get hurt more with flying pieces of glass. "Cover your eyes, quickly," Miss Love said, and then "Crash!" And when she hit the hole big enough the children inside had to crawl out, right over the sharp glass. And everyone was coughing and choking in the fumes.

"Is everyone out!!" Miss Love screamed. But there was no way to tell. The smoke was so bad we could only see the person right next to us, and there wasn't any time for Miss Love to run around and count us. We had to get out! "Please, children, can you tell if anyone is missing!" she cried.

I felt so dizzy I kept falling over. "Where's Donna!" I heard Lizabeth cry from behind me.

"I think she's in the front!" someone answered her.

"I can't breathe!"

"Help me, Miss Love!"

"We must get out of here right now, everyone!" Miss Love cried. "Come!"

There were a lot of us, but in the darkness and confusion we still couldn't tell if everyone was out. But we had to go! Holding on to each other in the smoke, we rushed back down the hallway away from there.

The fumes went on for a long time, but the further we went the less they were, and by the time we reached our first room the air was all right. We stumbled in and fell on the floor crying, and Miss Love stood there looking at us, counting to see if we were all there. Then "Donna!" she screamed. And a second later, "Steven! They are not here!"

She turned around and ran out into the hall again to go back and try to find them. But she would have died back there, and we'd all die without Miss Love, all of us. We need her! "NO!" I screamed. "Miss Love, stop!"

I jumped up and ran after her, out the door of the room and down the hall. But I didn't go far.

She was standing against a black wall just a few feet down the hallway from our room, holding herself up against it. I wondered about that, about how she could do that, since I was sure it was only a wall of black smoke from the cars, grown thicker and worse than before. But then I reached her, and it was not. It was a real wall.

And they were gone.

It's night again now, the night after.

And now there are only eighteen of us instead of twenty, and we're almost all hurt. Mark can't walk. We think he has a broken ankle. He fell when he climbed over two piled-up cars to escape. He crawled to get back to our room. Anthony can walk a little, even though his toe is gone, I guess because of his shoes, and Jeffrey's swollen ankle which he got falling off the fence is much better. And neither of them got hurt any more in the cars. Lizabeth, Karen, Joanne, Jackie and some others all have terrible bruises and cuts, and Peter and Yvette have black eyes. Kenneth got two teeth knocked out, and Paul is so dizzy he can't get anywhere without falling. He got a terribly hard hit on the head when we crashed, and just ignored it to help Miss Love. And then afterwards it started making him dizzy. Oh, and Lexi wasn't hurt anymore, but her nose is still terrible. The rest of us have injuries too, but smaller ones. Everyone keeps crying. Miss Love is all right, and I am too. And I'm not on guard, I'm just afraid to sleep. I'm afraid of nightmares, and I'm afraid of ghosts. I think children become ghosts when they die.

Saturday, April 29th

This, which I am afraid can only be unsatisfactory, is an attempt I must now make to understand and explain as well as I can what is happening to us. Where we are, what has happened, and what may become of us. Of why we are here I can do nothing but speculate, and Nadia has already described how we were brought to this place. It will not matter if I repeat things she has already said. I gave her this notebook to keep and she will continue to keep it, but two children are dead forever and I myself must speak.

I have kept careful track of dates, and we have been here now for 17 days. We were taken on a Wednesday, the

Miss Love was writing that but she couldn't finish. It was still the night after the cars happened, but I think almost morning, because I was the last on guard, and I was thinking it was almost day when it began. You can never really be sure, since no one has a watch and there are no windows in our rooms, but you learn to tell pretty well even without clocks or the sky to look at. And anyway, I was the last guard of the night so I knew the morning couldn't be too far away, and then the lights and noise and shaking started all over again. Everything was the same. Children running and crying, then Miss Love getting us all into one room together and telling us to try and try not to move, to resist as hard as we could and keep from moving, and then just like the last time we went out of control again. We huddled together in the terrible noises and shaking walls and flashing lights, and this time with those terrible cars to remember, and again we were pulled towards the door and out it. But it wasn't the cars this time. We were pulled and sucked down the hall, down, down, down, the hall getting wider and wider just like the first time, and suddenly there we were, and it was the same as the cars again. Except it wasn't cars. It was motorcycles.

But Kenneth has to take this book and write it in, because I can't write any more now, and Miss Love says he should. My head hurts too much, I'm hurt and I feel terrible.

I have to lie down now.

NADIA

P.S. I forgot to say since now other kids are going to write here too, I'm writing my name whenever it's me. Mostly, it still will be, Miss Love says.

This is Aliysha. Miss Love sent me to get the book from Nadia, and I did and I came right back but now she's not here, and I'm waiting for her to come back. I don't know where she is. But I can't look. She said she'd be here so she should be, but she will be in a minute. But I'm so scared. Then Kenneth is going to write all about the motorcycles but first Miss Love wants to write something, as soon as she gets here where I am and I give her the book. Why doesn't she come now. But all I have to say is Donna's *dead*, she *died*, and Lizabeth and I don't know what to do now and we're so scared that she's dead! I wish she'd come back! We miss her so much, poor Donna, and I

April 29th, continued

I found Aliysha hysterical. I returned only moments after she arrived with the book and she was crying hysterically, her whole body shaken with misery. When I came in, or no, when I walked up to her and put my arms around her and she looked up and saw me, for that was the first time she knew that I was there with her, she cried, "You weren't here, Miss Love! You told me you'd be here and you weren't!" But very quickly she broke down and sobbed in my arms, and now, having read the few lines she wrote here, it is clear Aliysha wept for the loss of Donna, and not anger at me. My poor children, how sorry I am for them.

But I must go on.

We were brought here on a Wednesday, the 12th of April, but by whom I do not know. I have no understanding of who imprisons us here, or why. But it is cruel. We are like children horribly, brutally punished without even knowing what we have done wrong.

We have lost two children, they are dead now. They are Donna Joffey, Age 10, of 172 11th Street, and Steven Black, Age 10, 196 2nd Street, both The City. They died either by automobile accident or carbon monoxide poisoning, but I am unable to tell which. They are dead. The details of their deaths have been recorded by Nadia earlier in this notebook.

I am responsible for the safety of all these children, as I was for the two we have lost. I am doing, and I will continue to do, my best. But I do not know whether it will be good enough, and I am filled with apprehension. We can only attempt to survive, to resist and to survive. I am teaching the children to resist. In every way, every moment of the day and night of their lives here. They are learning well, and I hope it will be enough.

I know there must be rational explanations for all the things that have happened, that are continuing to happen to us here. Mechanical tricks could very well account for some of the things, mechanically moving stairs, recorded screams, optical illusions to make walls appear to shudder and to move, perhaps even sleep-suggestion or mass hypnosis, to make us do things injurious to ourselves without in any way wishing to. Most of these things can somehow be explained. But even so, I have very thoroughly explored the possibility that we may all be mad, or that I may be, or that I may be dreaming, and I have come to see that one of these things may be possible. But there is no way now for me to know with certainty one way or the other. If this is a dream then I will know that when I emerge at the other end of it and begin to awaken, whenever that may be—this seems to have been going on for 17 days, and I am keeping actual count, one by one, as the days pass, but of course if I am dreaming it could be a matter of hours only, or even seconds, I believe. However, I am rather sure it is not a dream, and could not be one, if only for the reason that I do not dream. I have never dreamed, in all my life.

And if it is madness perhaps I will never come out of the other end of it, and I will never know.

Nadia, who I know reads everything in this notebook, will be very upset to hear me express these thoughts. But Nadia, please do not be disturbed, and do not any other of you children who read this either, and of course you all may. For I will tell you all that I am very much afraid this is not a dream, and not madness at all. And whatever it is, wherever it is, I am doing my best moment by moment to help every one of us here stay safe.

We have been here now for 17 days. For six of those days we had very little to eat, but since then we have had enough. Two children are dead, and many are injured. I do not know how much longer we will be here, or why we are here, or who the guards are. I can discover nothing. And so as I feared this attempt to explain our situation has after all explained nothing, but only expressed my own bewilderment.

There is one person here who is helping us: Raymond Amen, a prisoner himself, just as we are. He has told me his name and that he is eighteen years old. To him we owe Anthony's life.

The guards are a wall around us more solid and imperturbable than the real one, the high wire fence of which I know Nadia has spoken. It is a cruel fence, but the guards are far more cruel. Their inhumanity and utter lack of response to our helplessness are the elements of a far worse wall that tortures and frustrates us beyond bearing, until we would prefer any words of threat or hate to the silence which is all that they give us. That they are human beings is terrifying, for it does not seem possible, it is not tolerable. And yet we must tolerate it.

The children are bearing up to this inhuman nightmare place far better than even I might have hoped. They are wonderful, and I love them so much.

Kenneth will write of the motorcycles now.

H. Love

I miss Steven. He used to laugh too much and sometimes he was babyish but he was nice. He didn't fight much. He was my friend in school and my partner here. Now I have to stay with Greg and his partner, Paul, and Lizabeth and Aliysha don't have Donna anymore. Donna and Steven died in the car crash, but I'm supposed to write about the motorcycles.

I keep thinking about what it's like to be dead. I don't think it hurts or anything, and after you're dead for a while you can get born again. If we all didn't care so much about dying we wouldn't be so afraid of this place. But we are so afraid, and it's just because we don't want to be dead and we don't know what it's like to be dead, so we're scared of everything here, because we might get killed like Steven and Donna did. But Miss Love is Japanese and I'm Chinese, and we're not as much afraid as all the others, because we're not that scared of being dead. I want to go home though. Not because I'm scared, I just want to go home. My mother and father and brother and my little sister Patricia don't know what happened to me. I wish I could go home so they could see me and know I'm all right, and so I could see them too.

We just had to ride some motorcycles. It was worse than the cars, except nobody got killed. So I guess it wasn't worse. But it seemed worse to me, and more scary, at least I was more scared. And it was only one day after the cars, when someone *did* die, Donna and Steven died, and we kept expecting someone else to die too. We kept expecting *ourselves* to die, and I don't understand how no one did, I just don't understand. We had to walk down the hall like zombies again, and then get on black motorcycles and ride them. But nobody could steer them. They were really big and heavy, and none of our hands were strong enough to steer them, but we just got on them, like the cars, without deciding to, and they started. And they did it so quickly we all almost fell off at the very beginning. I was really scared then. I was supposed to be driving mine, but I couldn't and no one could. And then everyone did start falling off and almost getting killed, and thinking they were going to be, except some held on and crashed into other motorcycles or into walls. They went so fast, and hit the walls so hard! And they wouldn't stop, and we couldn't stop them. We didn't even know where the brakes were! So we just hung on until we fell off, and I don't know why nobody got killed. They were so big and black and fast we couldn't stop them, and they carried us on their backs racing like tanks and crashing into everything and we couldn't steer them or stop them or do anything about them, because they *had* us.

But what I don't know is how they can just go like that, all by themselves. Miss Love says we must not start believing it's magic, because there are ways to make things like that happen, even if we don't understand how. But that's more scary to me than anything, the way things can happen around here all the time all by themselves. It's like living in a spook house.

I was just remembering being home, and going for rides at amusement parks, when you get in a little car that's attached to the ceiling and drive all around trying to bump as many people as you can. That's fun. But those cars go because of electricity that you can even see and hear sizzling along the ceiling as you go, so there's nothing spooky about them, and besides they have big rubber bumpers, and you never get hurt, so it's fun. The cars and these motorcycles here are not fun, they're the worst things I ever saw in my life, and I never want to see them again.

Then we were finally all off the motorcycles, because they were all crashed and not going anymore, and we went back down the hall to here at last. We had to carry Mark, because he broke his ankle when it happened the first time, with the cars, and he can't walk. But you know what, he walked *to* the motorcycles! That's what I mean about strange things happening all the time. He walked there, but we had to carry him back here! So they made *it* so he could walk there, when the noises pulled us, and then it took four of us to carry him back, Jeffrey and Paul and Greg and me. And he kept crying all the way, about how he hurt his ankle again, and now he can't even crawl anymore, and I can still hear him crying, he still hasn't stopped.

I'm supposed to tell all the kids who got hurt on the motorcycles. Lexi's the worst. She fell off and hit her face and hurt her nose some more. She broke it when Jeffrey fell off the fence, and it hurt her so badly, and now it's worse than ever. Susanna and Yvette and Karen, and Aliysha and Paul and Jackie were all bleeding a lot, and Nadia held on and held on and then smashed into a wall headfirst and banged her head so hard she has a black and blue lump across her whole forehead. I don't remember what else. Nobody got killed. I'm okay. Everybody got so scared they're still shaking. The motorcycles really were much worse than the cars! They were, and I think it's mostly because you had to sit on top of them, not locked inside them like with the cars, and even so they *had* you and you couldn't get away. It was worse.

In case this book can get out I want to say one more thing.

Hello Mother, hello Father, hello Robert, hello Patricia.

KENNETH LING

We know it's dangerous, but Greg and Kenneth and I decided we're going to start spying on the guards. We'll probably do it very late at night. But we're not telling Miss Love. We can't, she would never let us do it. But we have to try something to get out, even if it's dangerous, we can't just stay here and get hurt and killed and not even try to find a way out! Even if it is dangerous! And maybe if we do it really a lot we'll find the way out of here. Because there has to be a way, even though there's no gate on the fence that we can see, and we checked it all around. But we came in, didn't we? Cars drove us in. And I'm sure there has to be a way out. We're going to do it as soon as we can.

I just remembered, if Miss Love reads the book now she'll find out! But it's okay, she probably won't have time to.

NADIA

This is Nadia again. I don't have anything to write, but I can't fall asleep and I just thought of a part I had in a play we did at school, that I can tell about. We did it in the auditorium, in front of half the school, a thousand kids. There are almost two thousand kids in our school. But it couldn't be for the whole school because they don't fit in the auditorium. So we did it for half, the fourth, fifth, and sixth grades. Then afterwards we would have done it for the younger grades too, but the teachers thought is was too old for them. It wasn't, but anyway we didn't get to do it.

We have a lot of trouble in school with drugs. Of

course, because the whole City has trouble with drugs, and we stand for The City. A lot of kids as young as eleven and twelve years old, almost the same as us, have been dying from overdoses lately, and we have a drug-education program in school to try to teach kids drugs are bad for them. But a lot of them in our school aren't learning, they're going on drugs. Nobody in our class, but a lot. The school is even worried about the real little kids, like the first-graders, who are only six years old. Not that they're using drugs or anything yet, but they know all about them, and they think they're good instead of bad. They even have a song they sing, with the same tune as "Fré-re Jac-ques":

> Mar-i-juana, Mar-i-juana,
> L.S.D., L.S.D.,
> Mr. Gaffney makes it,
> Everybody takes it,
> Good for you, good for me.

Then they giggle. Mr. Gaffney is the principal.

You always know which kids use drugs. They stand out, but anyway you see them in the bathroom all the time, smoking dope or even using needles. That's what they die from. If there's too much powder in the needle, or even if there's dirt on it sometimes. The teachers never catch them in the bathrooms though because teachers stay out of the children's bathrooms, and off the back staircases that the kids on drugs use too. They stay away because sometimes kids attack teachers. It's true.

The day before our picnic a teacher was found on a back staircase of another school, murdered. They caught a sixth-grader, and put him in jail.

None of us use drugs or anything because Miss Love is such a good teacher and she tells us not to, and why, and we love her so we listen and believe her, and we don't. But many kids do, and some die, so we have the drug-education program in our school, where they have assemblies with films, and policemen and other people like cured drug addicts come in and talk about every kind of drug, what it is and looks like and what it really does to you. We call them Dope Assemblies. They're once a week.

And once we put on a play at one of the Dope Assemblies. We wrote it ourselves. Miss Love said it was a morality play which is a play with a moral to teach you. Anyway, to start it the main character, a boy, Peter Borreca, went on stage and told all about his brother. His brother was a junkie at twelve years old. Peter was ten and he said he was sorry for his brother but glad he was the younger one because now that he'd seen what happened he was never going to touch any drugs himself. Then he went out, and his brother came in, who was played by Mark because he's big enough for twelve. Mark staggered in, fell down, got up, stole money from his mother, and went out again. Then we changed the stage to be a street corner, with pictures of buildings and a fence, and Mark came along, met the pusher, who was Paul, and paid him with his mother's money. Paul cheated him and went off the stage laughing, and Mark shouted after him and kicked over a garbage pail, and then he went off the stage too, but shaking and moaning.

After that we changed the stage back to the house again, and Mark came in. He tried to give himself the shot but the needle broke and he hurt himself. His arm started bleeding, of course with ketchup. He tried to give himself the shot with the broken needle, and hurt himself more. Then Peter, his brother, came home, except that Mark didn't see him, and Mark started running all around, throwing himself against the walls and down on the floor, acting crazy because he needed his shot, and then he took the needle, broke the glass part, and drank all the stuff that was in it. But Peter and the audience saw that he was drinking all the broken glass too, and Peter called the police for an ambulance. Gail, who was Peter and Mark's mother, came home at the same time the ambulance arrived, and as that act ended she was crying and running out the door to go to the hospital with Mark, and Peter said:

"My poor brother! And it could have happened to me if I was the older one, and I didn't know from seeing my brother! You'll never catch me on drugs!"

But there are two more acts in the play. In the second one some of Peter's friends start using drugs. He swears he'll never do it, but by the end he does. I come in in the third act. I am a teenager from a drug prevention program. I have been on drugs, but saved myself. I say to Peter:

"You, of all people! After you said you would never do

94

anything like that because you saw what happened to your brother! And where is he now? In the hospital again, and no one knows if he'll survive this time from an O.D.! Do you want that to happen to you too?" Peter says:

"But you don't understand, that won't happen to me. I'm careful! And good things happen with drugs too! You—I don't know, you don't feel bad then, or scared, and nothing hurts you, and—"

"Yes," I say then. "And does anything you eat ever taste any good any more? Do you even care if you ever eat or you don't?"

PETER: Well, not much I guess. But so what,

ME: Well do you ever go to the movies? Do you have any fun? Do you like to do *anything*?

PETER: Uh . . . well . . .

ME: Or do you steal money from your mother, and start to hate her, and all for the pusher!

PETER: No! I do not!

ME: Oh yes, you do! You know you do! And you're failing every subject in school and you're going to get left back. You keep falling asleep all the time, and today you almost got hit by a car because you didn't even know there was a street there! Come on now—let me help you!

We wrote the play ourselves. In the end Peter gets treatment and promises he's off drugs forever, and says when his brother gets home from the hospital he'll try to help him not go back to them either. But what I keep remembering is the part where he says, "But you don't feel bad, or scared, and nothing hurts you."

And if it wasn't for Miss Love, I'd wish—no, I wouldn't. Drugs still wouldn't be good. Because they might keep us from being scared so much, and sad, and from having bad nightmares, but if we took them we couldn't fight and *resist* anymore, and Miss Love says we must, we have to, everywhere and especially here, face and fight all our problems, and it's just no good hiding or using something like dope to pretend they're not there. Facing them is what resisting is, and what we always have to do to survive.

We found something funny out about the guards— funny-strange though, not funny-funny. Something disgusting and terrible. Kenneth and Greg and I were scared stiff to do it, but we made up our minds to, so when everyone was asleep except the ones on guard in our rooms, and they were practically asleep too, we snuck out. They didn't see us, and Miss Love didn't because she was in a different room from ours, with Mark, because he can't stop crying. Sometimes he stops for a little while, but he always starts again right away. He says it's because his ankle hurts him, but that's not why. It's because he's so scared. He's been doing it for days. Miss Love is very worried about him.

We had our shoes off, and crept down the stairs as quietly as we could. We weren't too worried about them shooting out to the sides because they never do on the way down, and they didn't. We got to the bottom and started walking around, looking for where the guards stayed when we were asleep, to try to spy on them without them seeing us.

It was easy. We walked around for a few minutes, and then we came to a door with a window in it, and a sign underneath the window that said:

Off-Duty Guardroom

Duty Regulations Do Not Apply

And when we looked through the window this is what we saw: a huge, giant room, with deep black couches and chairs and thick black rugs all over it, and cushions and pillows and big soft beds. We could see every part of the room. It had no windows at all, and it went on and on. There were a lot of different TV's, many of them facing the couches and easy chairs, and most of them were turned on to cartoons and old movies. And the room was full of guards. So it must have been very noisy, but we couldn't hear a thing through the door. But we could see their mouths moving, so we knew they were *talking*, they could talk! They were talking to each other, saying things!

And there was *food*: cakes and meat, delicious cookies and candy, bread, cheese, fruit, everything. And bottles and bottles of liquor and beer and wine, on different tables all over the room. And then on every table there were two or three dishes, with needles next to them, and white powder in them that I think was dope.

The room was filled with the guards, all with their uniforms open and at least partly off. The air was smoky from all their cigarettes, because most of them had cigarettes in their hands or mouths, some regular and some marijuana, skinny and twisted funny. And a lot of guards were eating and drinking and watching TV. But also many TV's were on with men in front of them who were not watching them, but were on the rugs and couches in front of them, naked, lying upside down to each other, with their mouths on each other, sucking each other like candy.

We turned and ran away. We found the stairs again and ran back up them and into my room, which comes first, and went all the way in the corner and hid. We didn't say anything, and I was crying and couldn't stop. Kenneth and Greg weren't crying at first but they looked ready to, and then all at once Kenneth started to, and soon he was crying so loud, "I want to go home, I want to go home," that Miss Love heard us and came in. Raymond was with her too.

We were the only ones in the room. While we were gone Lizabeth woke up and saw I wasn't there, and Aliysha, who was supposed to be guarding, was asleep by the door, and Lizabeth got scared and woke up Aliysha and they both went into another room to sleep. And it turned out that Miss Love wasn't in that room either, the one they went to, so they just figured I was with her, talking to her, and went back to sleep.

We couldn't stop crying even when Miss Love came. "Children, what is it?" she said. "Why are you crying, Kenneth? Nadia, what happened?"

But hearing Miss Love's voice just made me start crying harder. So Miss Love put her arms around me and Kenneth too, both at once, and smiled at Greg, and asked us to please try to be a little quieter so we wouldn't wake everyone else up. And we tried and slowly we were able to, and in the spaces between the rest of my sobs I told Miss Love everything.

Then I finished and said, "But Miss Love, what was that? I just don't understand what they were doing, why were they doing that? They were sucking each other like candy, they were sucking each other like lollipops!"

"That's not sex, Miss Love," Kenneth said, "sex is men and ladies! But they were all naked!"

"And some of them were turned around the right way too, and kissing each other, on the mouth!" Greg said.

"Are men supposed to kiss each other, Miss Love? I don't understand either, I thought it was only supposed to be men and women too!"

"All right, children, Nadia, and Gregory and Kenneth, I can see you are very upset by what you saw. Now tell me please, do you all know about sex between men and women?"

"Yes, we do know," I said, "but we don't understand about men and men."

"Well, you see, sometimes there is sex between men and men too."

"But that's bad, that's disgusting!" Greg shouted.

"Quietly, Gregory, please. Now tell me why you think that is so."

"Because it's disgusting, Miss Love! And isn't it bad?"

"Well, some people think it is. But do you know what, children? I am most surprised to hear that the guards do anything at all that means touching each other. Think what that means! They are human after all. That gives us more hope! If they eat, and drink, and make love to each other—"

"But is that what they were doing, making *love?*" Kenneth said.

"No, Miss Love, they weren't! Men can't!"

Miss Love was just about to answer when Raymond, who was just standing there listening, started talking instead.

"Do you know what?" We looked at him. "This is what I always think: how nice it would be if the idea that we were all brought up with was just to grow up and find someone to love, and that was all. It wouldn't matter who it was, a boy or a girl. You would just look at every person you met, everywhere you went, looking and hoping that they were the one. And whoever it was that you happened to love, well that was it. If you were a boy and you and a boy fell in love, then you couldn't have any children, that was all. It didn't matter, that was just the way it was. There were different ways of loving, and every child grew up knowing about them all. His parents taught him that when he was grown up he would just go out in the world and look until he found love, that was the first thing he had to do. And there were three different kinds of love, and two of them were possible for everyone. There was the love of a boy and a boy, a girl and a girl, and a boy and a girl. They were all just as valuable, they were just different, and most people didn't know when they started out which one they would have. They talked and wondered about it until they were old enough to go out and see. That's what I think about. I think that would be good."

Then he stopped talking and looked away from us, and Miss Love smiled at him. "That is a beautiful idea, Raymond. Did you hear of it somewhere? Or have you thought of it yourself?"

"Oh, I just thought of it," he said quietly, still half-turned away from us. "I think about it a lot sometimes. I never had any love at all, I wouldn't care who loved me. What difference would that make!"

"But Miss Love!" I said. "Do you think they *love* each other?"

"That is something I do not know, Nadia. But I do think that they *could*. Do you see?"

"I guess so."

"Good," said Miss Love. "And now we must all think about this, because it is very important: during the time they are on duty, and in charge of us and the other prisoners, they are one kind of person, but when they go off duty they are another. They must change when they go through their door. For even if they do not love each other, and are just having sex, even that is touching, and feeling, and so are eating and smoking and even using drugs, and all those things make them very different from the way they are at other times, because those are *human* things."

"Inside they have food and candy and dope and they touch each other and maybe even love each other."

"And outside they're mean and ugly and like machines!"

"And they don't touch anyone, except to hurt them! They hardly even see you, and they hate everyone!"

"No, outside they do not seem to love or hate," Miss Love said. "They seem not to have any human feelings at all. When we first arrived and I tried to speak to them it was as though I was not before them, as if they did not see me at all. But perhaps I must try again."

"Oh, don't do that," Raymond said.

"Why not, Raymond?"

"Just don't, you could be hurt."

"Yes, Miss Love," I said, "he's right, don't try! They're trying to make us die! That proves they hate us, and they'd hurt you!"

"But perhaps they would not hurt us if they could help it."

"You mean somebody *makes* them be like that?"

"I do not know," she said, "but perhaps, in the same way we are made to do things we do not want to do."

"But by who, Miss Love?" I said. "Who makes them?"

"That we do not know either, Nadia," she said. "And

now, children, you must promise me you will not go spying on the guards again. I must be able to trust you not to do it. Not you, and not anyone else. All right?"

"All right."

"Then goodnight," she said, "try to sleep now. Stay and sleep here for the rest of the night, all of you, and I will see you tomorrow. Goodnight."

"Goodnight, Miss Love."

"Goodnight."

May the 1st

Alexis Hill, Age 10½, 248 19th Street, The City. Died.

I haven't written anything for so long.

But I tried, and I couldn't. I couldn't. Then Miss Love said someone else would write it, she thought Greg would, but he didn't. No one could. So Miss Love said she would, but she just put in the name and address and date, and nothing else. And now it happened days and days ago, and still no one has told about it.

Lexi died.

She got pulled down underneath the ground. We were all just walking along outside, all of us together. We'd much rather stay in our rooms where it's safest but they don't let us, they come and get us and make us go outside. So we were walking along and after a while there were no guards anymore so we were talking and not thinking well. We should have known there was something funny, just because the guards were gone. But we didn't, so we were being careful of all the old dangers, the ones we knew about, the fence and the pond with piranha and their taking control of us and even just the guards, themselves, in case they should come back suddenly, but we were not watching out carefully enough for any new dangers or traps. And we were just walking along and suddenly the ground felt different, horrible and soft, and all of a sudden we couldn't move anymore. No, first we just couldn't move, and then we slowly started sinking down into the ground, the ground began pulling us down into it. We cried to Miss Love for help, but she couldn't help us, she was stuck too. She was struggling and struggling to move, and then she gasped, "It must be quicksand!" Then everybody was screaming and crying, "I can't move! It's got me! I can't get out, help!" All of a sudden Miss Love shouted, "NO!"

As frightened as we were, we all stopped and tried to turn our heads around to see her.

"No!" she kept shouting, "this will not happen to us, no! I will not allow it! You will move, children, move, use all your strength and slowly move! We will not let this happen to us!"

It wasn't our strength, it was hers: we all got out—all except Lexi. Lexi didn't.

It was because all the rest of us took Miss Love's strength and used it, but Lexi wouldn't. She was always so funny and quick, I mean to do anything, and she liked to do everything herself. She thought she could do it herself. But she couldn't. So we all moved slowly and strongly, along with Miss Love, and slowly began to get out, but Lexi Hill tried to go fast, she used up all her strength trying to go fast and she never moved at all. Her body twisted and twisted but it didn't move an inch, except to go down. Slowly, we all got out. And when we were out, we couldn't reach her. It was too late. Miss Love tried to get to her, but she couldn't. No one could reach her, and she kept going down.

Everything is strange. Everyone's been acting strange since Lexi died. We don't feel so scared anymore, and that's strange. Miss Love says it's resignation. Or else she said recognition, I don't remember which one. And she says it's terrible, and we have to make ourselves stop, because it's just what they want. We walk around all the time as if we're in a trance or something, and Miss Love says we'll walk right into danger or death if we keep going on this way, and she keeps trying to cheer us up. But she's really the same, Miss Love feels the same as we do. And sometimes she talks to Raymond instead of us. I think it's because he's more grown up. It must be hard for her to only have children to talk to, us. She loves us but she's tired of just having us around, or at least a little, I bet.

NADIA

iii

Happy Thought

The world is so full of a number of things,
I'm sure we should all be as happy as kings.

—R. L. Stevenson

May the 20th

I do not know what to do. I have taken this book from
Nadia. I think I may have been wrong, and after all it
may not have been good for her to have it, and write in it
so much. It kept her very busy for a while, but since a
week after Lexi died she has written only one page—but
oh, how she reads! How they all read! They read Nadia's
and my words in this book over and over, and it is not
good for them, for they worry so. Too much, too much.

109

I have told them all that I must keep the book for a while now. And so perhaps now I will use it, for I too have a need to write in it, and perhaps my need is even greater than the children's was, or still is, for I think they will need to write in it again. And we have only this one book. But still I must use some of the space.

For I do not know what to do. I cannot believe that we are to remain here, but so it seems. I have kept a careful record of time since we were brought here and now I wish I had not, how much better it would be if I had not! For now I know with certainty that we have been here for more than one month. It is nearly the summer now, it is May the 20th!

But it is not possible. How can this be? All of this? Where is this place, where the weather never changes, and where is the world? I look through the crossed wires of the fence surrounding us, and I see nothing! And at first I told myself that was not so very unusual, and this simply must be far out in the country somewhere, so there would be nothing one would see. But no. For I must be as rational as I can, and some things simply do not seem possible. The nothing that is through the fence is truly that, it is *nothing*. I cannot make out anything. Is it fields, or wasteland? I see no trees, I see no grass. I see no cars, and no form of life or movement whatever. There are no planes in the sky, there is only nothing. But can that be? There is no place like this in the world, there is no space for it. And so how can it be? Are we really here, real people in a real place? Or are we instead mad or dreaming?

I do not know, how can I know?

It is one month and I have not yet awakened from this madness. Raymond swears he has been here for years. When I question him his answers seem like fiction only, they could not be true. He says he has been here for eight years! How can I believe that? He says a few of his former classmates are among the guards, and the rest are dead, and we too will all be dead soon! Surely, and soon. "But who are they?" I ask him. "Who is keeping us here!" I ask and ask him, but he does not tell me, he says that he does not know. Then how will I ever find out? "But how is it that you are alive then, Raymond, and not a guard?" I ask him. "Because they were always so sure I would die!" he answers, "but somehow I didn't, and then it was too late."

"What do you mean, too late?"

"To be taken for the guards! When you've been here and alive for a while, I don't know how long, two or three months, they try to get you for the guards. They get the ones they want, and the rest of the class, the ones who don't go, die very soon after that. They all die. But of course they don't know it until it happens. But when the ones still alive from my group, my class, went to the guards, and then all the others died, somehow they forgot me. And I didn't die. So they started waiting for me to die. They're still waiting for me to die."

"But you could not become a guard after that?"

"Oh no, they only give you one chance. I mean it's really like two or three chances, but all at once, around the same time, and after that they never change their minds. And anyway, they wouldn't want me. They pick which ones they want, and I'm in the group of the ones they wanted dead. Except I'm still alive."

"And your classmates, those who are guards? Do they never speak to you?"

"Speak to me? I don't even know which ones they are!"

"But how could that be? I do not understand."

"They're changed, that's all. And I don't know who they are." He would not say more than that.

And this Raymond, I am so disturbed about him. He is the only person here to help me, and he seems so doomed. I cannot understand how he has not died here, and I fear that he still will, and he is my only support. The children I cannot call support. I am their support. They depend on me completely, and I can never fail them. And already three of them have died! Steven, Donna, and Lexi, and Mark I fear may die, for he does nothing but cry, and he will not eat. A bite or two each day, and a little water, and that is all.

But on reflection I am left wondering only why so *few* of us have died! Why only three? The death traps they set for us are so truly terrible, how have the rest of us escaped? Are we being kept alive only to be teased and tortured? Or is it because some of us must survive to go to these guards, to become guards ourselves! Guards!

Nadia continually asks me for this book. She says she needs it so badly, but I do not think she should have it to write in or read any longer, I do not think any of the children should, and I do not know what to do about it.

There is too much in it of dying. Oh, I do not know what to do about anything, anything.

May 22nd

The time of my wondering has come to its end. Now they are getting down to their vicious business. Tiring of waiting for us to be caught in one or another of their traps, they simply locked the doors and fed poisonous gas into our rooms, slowly, insidiously in the night, and oh I think they did not want any of us for the ranks of their guards, for we would all surely have died.

But Raymond came. He heard us choking and screaming, and he came, and with wildcat's strength and beating with his feet and fists on our doors and locks he broke open the doors of four of our rooms.

Three children were in the room whose door he could not open, and all of them are dead. We heard them struggling and coughing and crying and then we heard nothing. In the morning the door was unlocked and their bodies gone.

There are no funerals here. I do not know what they have done with the bodies. We saw a graveyard once, when we first arrived, a graveyard of children, with small, narrow mounds, so many of them, but we have not seen it again. I do not know what I will tell their parents, if ever I should see them again.

DEAD
Mark Toberman, Age 10, of 242 1st Avenue,
Peter Borreca, Age 10½, of 116 11th Street,

Paul Weaver, Age 11, of 86 9th Street,
all The City.

It is Mark I am the most unhappy about—not because I loved him more than the others but because he was so afraid, and all his fears came true.

And yet, perhaps it is better that he is dead! Now it is over for him, all this, this terrible place, he does not need to be afraid any longer. For he was so afraid. He was in such terror of everything, breathless and crying with fear for days without end. And when the doors shut and locked and the fumes began pouring in our rooms the horror and panic were unendurable, and I think and think of Mark, separate from me, in another room, for how many long, desperate minutes before he died. For we knew at once we would not be able to get out. I have spoken of it with the children and it was the same in all the rooms, terror and despair, choking and suffocating us along with the poisonous black fumes.

And I was asleep: only for a moment, but I was asleep when it began. But even awake, I do not think I would have been able to stop it, because the children who were on guard in all the rooms saw and heard nothing until suddenly the doors had shut and locked all by themselves, just as it was in the shelter in the park when we were captured. The doors just shut and locked us in, and the poison began to fill the air.

And then we did not die, I did not die and the children in the room with me and in three other rooms did not die. Three did. Three more children are dead. The rest of us were saved. But will Raymond be able to help us the next time? Will we be able to help ourselves?

My despair is so great. It is only a matter of time before we are all dead. They wait for us to die. That is all.

May 23rd

They have tried it again, and we are not dead. That trick will not work again, they will have to find others. And oh they must have wondered why it did not work, when they unlocked the doors and found us still breathing, and had to go away again and let us live. For that is what happened. And it did not work because for hours yesterday, thinking they might repeat it, we worked secretly on the doors of our rooms, always with our bodies placed so they would not see, and carefully, so carefully, we made a way to breathe. Only in two rooms though, we are staying together now, now they will see us resist.

We thought first of removing the locks entirely, so that if they did try it again we would be able to get out. But we decided against that, thinking they would surely discover it and find some way around it. We needed something secret, that they would not know about and that could remain hidden, but that would be waiting to help us when we needed it.

And so we made air holes in the doors of our two rooms. We worked with the back of my nail file and loosened the screws of the door-hinges until we could extract them any time, quickly, with ease, and then gently re-

115

placed them. There are three hinges on each door, and three screws on each hinge. We made all but one on each hinge removable, and so had six small airholes on each door.

And evening came, night came, and I did not sleep, and Anthony, on guard in the other room, did not sleep, and even so the doors shut and locked, so quickly we were helpless to stop them. And then the fumes began. But we held our mouths in turn to the air holes and breathed, sucked and breathed through the holes, and we did not die.

Raymond did not come, for this time he did not hear us. They took great care that he would not, I am sure. But they do not know our resistance, they do not know that we will not die.

It would be dangerous for the guards to read this book. But I do not think they know about it, and I do not think they really care to. They simply carry out motions, efforts to kill us, and succeed or do not succeed, and do not care. They do not have cunning, only purpose. Even so, it would be dangerous, but we guard this book carefully. It will be all right.

This is not possible. It is impossible, it cannot be. I am a woman, I am twenty-six years old, and this cannot be. Raymond is eighteen. He is a child.

No, he is not.

And now I am using this notebook for my personal diary. But I must, I cannot help it. I have no one but the children to talk with, and I cannot speak to them of this. And it is inconceivable. I must write it all down, and then try to understand what I have written, what has happened.

The children were in their rooms and already sleeping, all of them in just two rooms. We keep together now, in our fear and misery, all the children and I. I try to keep them occupied and busy and their minds away from this place, but it is ridiculous even to hope that I might succeed, when any moment any terrible and inconceivable thing whatsoever could actually begin to happen, for oh yes, here it could. And so we use only two rooms now, and during the day only one. I tell the children stories, all the stories in the world, and we all stay together until night, when we separate because we cannot sleep all in one room, we do not fit. Otherwise we would.

We try to pretend we are elsewhere, perhaps in a strange school somewhere. We do not speak of dangers, and we try not to speak of deaths. When a child must speak of his fears I take him aside. And they fear everything now. The lethargy that we all fell into at Lexi's death disappeared with the deaths of Mark and Paul and Peter, and now they fear everything, real things and imagined, for what difference is there between them? Here, where the real things seem most imaginary. They tell me their fears of impossible things, and I cannot truthfully assure them that those things will not happen here!

Then what can be wrong with me, to become even to a

degree immersed in myself? How can I even think of such a thing as love when the children need me so desperately!

Raymond is nearly a decade younger than I, but taller and stronger. I can lean on him, he can bear my weight. He can support me, physically, emotionally. His skin is warm and smooth to my touch. And I have touched it! He was waiting for me last evening outside our door—it is day now and I am writing, attempting to understand it. I came out of one of the rooms and saw him, and he looked at me so strangely.

"Raymond, what are you doing there?" I said. "Did you want to talk to me? Why did you not come in the room?"

"Are all the children asleep?"

"Yes, as asleep as they can be. They are dreaming so much now, tossing and crying all night long. They spend all their nights dreaming. But what is the matter, Raymond? You look so strange."

"Oh, Miss Love," he said, "I had to see you, I had to. Please, help me! I wish I were dead! I was born to die, why am I still alive!"

"But Raymond, what do you mean? You cannot really want to die?"

"Oh yes, I do if I'm going to anyway, and I am! This waiting, always waiting—listen, Miss Love, I was *born* to die! The moment I was born, I was ready to die! My mother told me the doctor had to smack me three times before I would breathe, and then I cried so long they had to put me in a lukewarm bath to calm me down and stop me! And then I started to grow up, and I tried to die, I kept trying to, I tried to by not eating anything, but they wouldn't let me do that, they made me eat. So as soon as I was big enough to crawl, I crawled to the oven and burned myself! I wanted to burn all up, but they came too soon! That's where all these scars come from, look." And he showed me a long line of red scars all the way down his arm.

"Oh no," I cried, "that is terrible! But it was an accident, Raymond, you did not do it on purpose!"

"Oh yes I did, I really did, Miss Love. They go all the way down my side too! I was trying to die! Everywhere I could crawl to, everywhere I could get to, I got there to try to die. I slipped under the water in the bathtub so many times trying to drown myself they finally had to stop giving me baths. And I was sick, too, I've been sick every day of my life!"

"You are certainly thin for someone as tall as you are," I answered, smiling as I did, "but you are also strong, you know, and you do look all right. I do not think you are sick. How old are you, Raymond, did you tell me you are eighteen?"

"Yes, my birthday was just before you came. I keep track of time, you know. I steal pencils, and I have all the dates of all the years I've been here written on the walls in my room. They're everywhere you look. So I know it was my birthday just before you came here, and I'm *eighteen* now, and oh, Miss Love, I don't understand why they don't kill me, why don't they! No one else is ever alive here this long! My mother gave me a birthday party when I was ten years old, and that was just before they got me here, I've been here all the time since then! We had everyone in my class at that party, thirty children. I told her I didn't want everybody but she just called up all the mothers, and then everybody came, because they all thought it was going to be a terrific party, something special! And she didn't have anything, just some stupid cake and soda, and they all hated it. They hated me, and if she'd invited ten people and they'd known it was just a regular party, two might have come, or none. So that was the party—terrible. And on my ninth birthday, the year before that, I was in the hospital having my appendix out. And I was also undernourished. I've always been. The doctor couldn't understand it. He asked my mother to show him her welfare card, to check if we got enough money for food. Welfare! Very funny, that wasn't why, we were never on welfare. It was because I didn't eat. 'But Raymond is starving, Mrs. Amen!' that doctor said. So my mother started sobbing, 'He just won't eat! I've tried everything!' And then the doctor patted her on the shoulder and said not to cry, it was all right, but that I was a very sick boy. As if she didn't know it! And I needed help—and oh, Miss Love, now I've been here for eight years! I've never had anything good!"

"I know, Raymond," I said, "it is terrible." And I reached out to touch his arm, to comfort him, but once again his skin was so warm I could not stop myself from jumping back in surprise. It did not feel like the skin on

120

one's arm. It was more like the soft, warm, protected feeling that the body has underneath clothing.

"Raymond," I said quickly, "I will tell you what I think: I do not believe you are sick at all. In fact I think you must be particularly strong and well and clever, or else how could you have survived here for so long? How could you have survived here at all, if you were not especially strong?"

"I don't know," he cried. But then his face flushed, and he looked away from me and said, so softly and quietly I almost did not hear it, "I had sex, with a guard. At first I thought he—it's terrible, but I think he protects me. I still, sometimes . . ." Then he looked right at me again. "But I wouldn't care that it was a man, I wouldn't even care that it was a guard, if he cared about me! But he doesn't! He likes to have sex with me, that's all! But I'm not really like that either, Miss Love, I'm not!"

I did not know what to say, and I reached out once again and touched him very lightly. And suddenly he moved and his arms were around me, and he was holding me and would not let go.

"What are you doing?" I cried. "Raymond, please, do not . . ."

"Oh Miss Love, please, I have to hold you or I'll die! I'll die of being alone! Just let me hold you, Miss Love, please, I love you!"

"Raymond . . ." I tried to move away from him, but he would not let me go, he pulled me even closer and tighter, holding me and whispering, "I can love you, Miss

Love, I can, it can be better for us here. I can make it better, I can take care of you, and you can take care of me, please, oh please, please."

"But Raymond," I said at last, trying to resist him, and the temptation I felt to give in to him and love him, "Raymond, I am so much older than you, you are still a child!"

"No, I'm not!" he cried. "I feel older than you! I never felt strong before but I do now! And I am! Oh Miss Love, Miss Love," he said, and he kissed me.

And I kissed him back. And held him and caressed him, and was held by him, and caressed, and I felt myself loving him, closing my eyes and holding him, letting myself go and being held, with his long, thin, soft, quick hands stroking me, stroking me, making me feel so good, better than I have felt for such a very long time.

The children are very worried. Nadia is ill. I do not know what illness she has—fever, but why? And it is worse than it should have been, than it would have been had I been able to keep her quiet, resting and quiet as she should be. But no, I could not. They drive us out, they will not leave us alone. Three times now, three nights in succession, voiceless and all in black the guards have come up the spiral stairs and stamped into our rooms to awaken us with noise and blows, and drive us out, down the stairs and outside into the blackness of night. Moment by moment, we do not know what to expect, what danger, what threat.

Oh but we are almost veterans, sometimes now we can

even recognize the pitfalls and avoid them in time. Others are not so fortunate. Last night two more died in the quicksand, children. Not my children, others. We had seen them before but never spoken to them, we may not. We could not get near them to help them, the guards held us back.

Nadia grows worse in the frightful air.

Raymond has told me all about himself now. I do not neglect the children. I spend all their waking time with them, helping them, sharing the food, trying to keep them safe and occupied, and I have told Raymond of their need and that I belong to them. But at night, when they sleep and I do not, then I am with Raymond, and we sit together and talk, whispering so the children will not wake. I do not have them keep guard any longer. It frightened them too much, and now there is really no need for it, since we use only two rooms, side by side, and Raymond and I stay all night just outside their doors, or inside one of them and in sight of the other, and guard them both at once. I sleep a little during the day, only a little, when it is safe and nothing is happening and the children seem for a moment not too worried. When there is nothing, for a moment, to fear. But all night we sit outside their rooms, and guard them.

And we talk. We talk and talk, and we kiss and caress each other—and sometimes, in the deepest part of night, we love. Oh, it is a very simple and quiet and gentle kind of loving, for we must do it secretly, from the guards and from the children, but it is love, and warmth, and softness. And afterwards we sit again, all alone in the dark, always touching each other, and we talk.

I have a fever. A hundred and three or a hundred and four, I know it. Why can't I write here anymore, Miss Love? You have to let me. My head aches and I have a fever, it isn't fair

Nadia had the book again. I left it for only a moment and she rose from her bed and took it. She is ill, she burns with fever. But Nadia, please, you must give me a little time! Only a little, but please allow me a few moments of my own, from you, and your needs, and Kenneth and his and Aliysha's and Karen's and all the others —but oh, forgive me, children—I am like a mole, finding myself deep in a new warm burrow of my own, out of the cold, and Nadia, please, in this terrible place we are in, will you please allow me to burrow deeply and desperately for a moment only, only a moment, in the nights, in the dark nights, and still I will give you the days—

Fourteen of us remain. No new traps, no poison for a while. Waiting, only waiting. While I burrow.

May 30th

Raymond's father was a homosexual. Not his real father (he had none, his real father deserted him when he was an infant), but his uncle, his mother's brother, a wicked woman's wicked brother. Raymond sees his uncle-father's countenance in every guard's face—because of

124

the evil—though the guards are so hard, and his uncle was soft, he could not have been softer—

Raymond's uncle was his father because he acted so. He punished Raymond and rewarded him, whipped him and praised him, led him by the hand to the zoo and church and concert hall, whipped him when they returned home because Raymond had not sat still enough, had fidgeted, Raymond says whipped him and whipped him because Raymond would not cry, whipped him until he did. His mother ignored all of it. Raymond, his uncle, the whippings.

He, this uncle-father, had no coat. Raymond remembers and remembers this. He had a cape instead: a deep blue, full, flowing, skirted, swirling, English bobby's cape, and I too can see it, Raymond remembers and speaks of it until I do. He wore it fall, winter, spring, always, draped over his shoulders languidly, and always swirled it on by whirling it over his shoulders like a master of ceremonies. And his hair: platinum blond, dyed, Raymond told me. "Platinum?" I asked, amazed.

"Oh yes. Bright, white yellow. Dyed blond."

"Did he dye it himself?"

"Yes, in the bathroom. My mother used to help, but then she wouldn't do it anymore, and I had to. I wore rubber gloves that were hers. They were so big for me my hands wobbled loose inside them. I had to spread the peroxide all over his head, but not let any of it get on the hair further out: only at the roots. If I let it get on any of the long hair it turned red."

125

"And he did not like that?"

"He hated it! It got him furious. And the peroxide smell was so horrible! I'd start to faint again and again, but then I wouldn't, I'd keep gasping for breath and turning my head to the side, away from the fumes to gulp air, until I had to turn back. And the fumes burned my eyes too, and hurt me.

"His name was Jonathan. Jonathan with the bright yellow hair. And you know what he did? He was a hairdresser! He dyed his hair at home so all the people at the beauty parlor would think it was real! And you know what he *wanted* to be . . . ?"

Raymond was speaking very fast, so excited, his skin and eyes shining and his hands moving through the air.

"A priest! He really wanted to be! He went to church all the time and he hated taking me, he said I spoiled it for him, but my mother made him. And he was always walking around the room swaying and nodding his head and mumbling as if he was saying prayers. And you know what else? He had a priest's outfit! I don't know where he got it, but it was just like a real one, it wasn't like a costume or anything, it really looked real. It was a real long black priest's dress that went all the way down to the floor, with tiny black buttons from its neck to its feet. It took him five minutes to get it buttoned. And he had a big white collar with frilly lace around the edge, that went on top of the black dress. He'd always shave first, put it all on, and then put on shiny black patent leather boots he had too, even though only a little bit of their toes stuck out from underneath the gown. And then, all dressed up like that, he'd march around and around the room, prancing and smiling the way he thought priests smiled. All black and white, with his pink face and the golden hair on top, in little ringlet-waves that he made with his fingers. And he marched around and around. And sometimes the cats we had, two black-and-white cats, followed him. I don't know why, maybe they liked the way he pranced, or the way the black skirt of the gown swished across the floor or something, although they never hit at it or anything, as if they were stalking it. I don't know. But anyway, he didn't mind it at all, he liked them following him around, and he didn't think it looked ridiculous. But it did! They were black cats with white throats, white lacy throats, because of the way the white fur met the black and ended in little dips, and they looked like miniatures of him. They'd walk all around with him, sometimes in front, sometimes in back, sometimes going right between his legs, under his skirt from the front and then out the back again. He loved those cats a lot more than me. He talked to them. He was Father Jonathan and they were his flock. He pretended they were people who had come to his church, and he preached sermons to them!

"Then sometimes friends of his came. But he didn't care if they saw him like that, they were all like him anyway. Not that I knew what it was then, but I figured it out as soon as I was old enough, I figured it out *here*. That's for sure, I remembered and I figured it out. All queers. And I almost got to be one too. My *father*."

"But not your real father, Raymond."

127

"But the only one I ever had! I never saw the real one, and I never heard about him either, my mother never told me a single thing about him! Jonathan told me I used to have a father, but he left, and that's all I ever knew! And we lived with my uncle, and I didn't call him Uncle Jonathan, I called him Jonathan, and he was always dressing up like a priest and calling himself *Father Jonathan*. You see?"

June the 4th

And now another.

The guards drove us out again. It was the dark night, they drove us out, and we were walking so carefully, fearful of that very thing, the ground that could without warning begin to open, when suddenly many more guards came and began chasing us. They are not human beings, I do not know what they are. They came running behind us, striking us hard, some with the butts of their guns. Gail was hurt, they struck her with such terrible force we heard a bone crack, the sound it made loud and sickening. We were stumbling and trying to run, pursued and beaten, I half-carrying Nadia who is so ill, when I heard the crack and then Gail screamed and fell to the ground, and I let go of Nadia and spun around and tried to go back to her, but they stopped me, would not let me go, and the ground had her, took her—

These things I am saying, writing, they are not possible—

After she was gone they pursued us no longer. Our arms around each other, weeping for Gail and her long, shining hair, her brown hair, how she would comb it and comb it, sleek and shining with light, always asking for my comb, Gail—

Twelve children remain.

These things are not happening, they could not

I tell Raymond about myself too. We do not talk all the time, but we talk a lot, in the night, and it is so good, for me, for him, so very good, we need to talk to each other so much, nearly as much as we need to love each other.

I tell him about—not my childhood, that is for him to tell. I tell him about my children. These children, and how it was before we came here. What the children are to me, all my life—until now, for now Raymond is my life too. And I tell him I have always loved my children, because I do and because it is my job, my name and my job, much more than just to teach them, to teach them to love.

Mark, who is dead, oh poor Mark, when school began last fall, and I saw him for the first time, the moment all the new children were in the room and the confusion over, and I looked around me at all their new faces, my children for one year. They assign children to their classes in our school according to intelligence, and I am given the brightest children of all, so I knew Mark had to be very intelligent to be in my class. But you would not have known it to look at him. He was such a big boy, and yet soft, so soft. There was no strength in him anywhere, from his thick, dull hair to his eyes, cow-brown, and his pallid skin and big, soft mouth and his chin, chin going nowhere, chin running away backwards. And his arms and hands always off in the wrong directions, out to the sides or wavering in front of him, anywhere but where they should have been, and tears shining in his eyes all the time.

But why am I talking of my children at all? To Raymond, and now writing it too, and so saying it for a second time! I thought I needed to be away from them for a while. Ah, but I do not, I do not, it is the danger I need to be away from, for a little bit, and the fear, the responsibility of all of them *here*, it is this *place*. But no, not my children.

On the first day I always settle them in. They sit, talking with each other, watching me and wondering, and I wait until at last they are very, very quiet. Then I begin to speak, but softly, so softly they must listen hard to hear me. I tell them my name; they stare at me, they cannot say it. And so I smile and tell them, "In English it means—well, more than one thing, but the nicest is love, that is one of its meanings. Some of my classes have called me Miss Love, and I do not mind that." And I look around at them and say, "Well, tell me, what do you think? Can you say that?"

Of course the children like this very much, though at first some of them are embarrassed by it and find it hard to say. But they soon enjoy this name and are happy to call me by it. And this class too. But oh, Mark, I thought his tears would really flow, they filled his eyes so. He could hardly control himself, and at what? A smile and the word love? They come from such terribly busy homes, most of the children, where there is never time for loving them enough. That is why love is what they need most, not just learning, and what I must give them. But it was hard with Mark. He needed love so badly that I could not give it to him except in very small, measured amounts, or he collapsed. It had to be mixed, with strength and sternness, like a drugstore prescription. I found that out at once.

It is so sad that children must go unloved. I have always wondered about it. I do not think parents intend to neglect their children, they just cannot find the time for loving them. They must fight too hard, too much of the time. To find jobs—more than one, as one does not provide enough money to live on, and so usually both parents must work—and then to keep them; to find apartments, and keep them, when there are none to find. And they cannot leave The City to find a better place to live in, it is too hard, they would have to find the jobs and apartments all over again. There is nothing to be done. And with all these things to do and to worry about, how could parents have time for loving their children? And so they do not, most of them really do not. And so I do, and I always will.

Nadia's fever has grown worse. She is unconscious. I do not even have spare water for her to drink, or to smooth on her to cool her fevered skin. I have nothing.

I went to the guards for help. There is no point. It was midmorning; I told the children I would be right back, and left. Down the stairs, stepping over the seventh each time, then turning the corners trying to remember the way Nadia said she and Kenneth and Gregory went when they found the guardroom. And I was stopped by no one, and I found it.

All the things the children saw—I saw them. They are true, they were not exaggerating. It was day instead of night, and so there were fewer guards in the room than Nadia described, but all those who were there were— pleasuring themselves, in one way or another, sexual and otherwise, but all of the ways physical, slow, and continuous, with their bodies moving and their *faces* expressive and alive, far from their usual masks! But it was silent, or rather the noise they must have been making was not passing through the door, as the children said. I stood peering through the window in the door for a long time, nearly hypnotized, before I remembered Nadia and knocked.

There was no answer, and I stood stupidly waiting and knocking repeatedly, getting no answer and finding myself drifting and beginning to stare at them once again, in a way so unreal, until I would pull myself up and knock again—and receive no answer, and begin to drift. I could not stop. But I could hear the sound of my own knocking, and feel my knuckles hitting against the glass and the door, so I knew I was there, and not upstairs and only dreaming or imagining that I was. But no one answered. At last in desperation I reached down and touched the doorknob, to turn it.

I could not believe the shock.

I lay on the floor flat on my back: the knob had electricity running through it. It had taken me and thrown me down so violently that my body felt broken and boneless. At once two guards, but fully dressed and with their expressionless faces, rushed at me. The door to the room never opened.

"Please," I cried, "please help me, you must, a child is dying, fever is consuming her! She is so sick, you must have something to help her, even some aspirin, anything!"

But they did not answer. Instead they pushed at me with their gun-butts, prodding me until somehow I was up. I stood giddy from shock before them and begged, "Please, you must understand, please help me," but even as I spoke they were pushing me backwards.

"*No!*" I screamed, "you are human beings! *Help me*, a child is dying! She has never done anything to hurt you, oh please, please!" But then I had lost control of myself, and reached out to hit them, tear at them, hurt them any way I could. My hands struck them, my nails found *blood*, and they did not react. They did not flinch, they just kept advancing, advancing and pushing me back.

Then there were the stairs, the seventh, I was careless and stepped on one but fell to my knees and saved myself, there was noise, flashing light, I am bruised and bleeding.

There is no point.

Nadia is the same: still alive. I can do nothing but try to bring her fever down, I must find some way to bring it down. I am going to begin fanning her.

There is no point.

I told Raymond this: I grew up in silence. Both my mother and my father were deaf-mutes. They told me of their love for me with their eyes and with their hands and fingers, but they could not speak, and I could not believe them. I have been imagining all my life the sound of my mother's voice, my father's voice. I have needed the sound of their voices, speaking to me, caressingly. As soon as I could I ran from my home, for their silence hurt me, it hurt me so.

Now I cannot stop speaking, sound is the point of all meaning to me. Slow and soft, Raymond, speak to me, and then touch. I can live the sound of Raymond's voice forever.

Nadia regained consciousness for a moment tonight.

"Miss Love."

"I am here, Nadia dear."

"Miss Love—"

"Oh, Nadia, do not try to speak now. You are still so ill."

"I'm so hot, Miss Love."

"I know." I laid my hand on her cheek.

"Hold me, Miss Love."

I put my arms around her.

"Miss Love . . . I love you."

I lay down beside her, and put my arms around her.

"Miss Love, do you love me? Do you love Raymond better than us?"

"Oh, Nadia, I have so much love, I have enough love for all of you and Raymond."

"Hold me, Miss Love."

It is night, still, slow-soft. Around us there is nothing —walls, darkness, fences, and the world nowhere. Sleeping, dreaming children, thrashing in their covers. Nadia's fever abating, perhaps, at last. Around us nothing. Night. What country are we in? What country is this?

June the 14th

I do not know how to go on.

I cannot believe this, any of it. How can I write it? Is it fiction I am making up? I cannot turn the pages of this book any longer, and write in it, and read the things that are in it, for they are mad!

And I must.

Once again we were led in the dark, in the night, outside, and were forced by the guards with white and terrible faces to the edge of a pool we knew must contain vicious fish because as we approached it Anthony screamed, "No! It's the pool!" and tried to run back through the lines of guards and escape. He was shoved brutally along with us instead, and then suddenly all of us were pushed into the water.

It was not deep. Most children were touching the bottom and standing, and smaller children were hanging onto bigger ones. But the water was full of our fear and we imagined schools of terrible fish sweeping through it towards us. Nadia, so weak, kept sinking under the water while I tried to hold her and children all around me screamed *help me! help me!* And my mind was crying *Raymond, Raymond*, while my arms held Nadia and

135

held Aliysha, and Anthony thrashed and screamed his pain from the fish of his terrible memory.

Then a moment of respite, one moment only, a lull in the terror as I looked up and saw the guards were gone. They had stayed at the edge of the pool to keep us from trying to climb out, had already pushed several struggling children back in, but now they were gone, and I saw it and at the same time realized there were no fish, and spoke to the children then, quickly, with joy and relief, "Children, just swim or float to the edge now, or see if you can stand, it is all right! You can do it, look, we will be all right now, come, climb out, the guards are gone and there are no fish!"

And they listened and believed, and began to try to reach the side. And then terror again:

"Look out!" The madness, the unbelievable, over our heads a thing, a cover, of wood, heavy, the size and shape of the whole surface of the water was descending, slowly, coming down on top of us, we could not lift it by pushing with our hands or heads and we were thrashing again, desperately struggling to get out before it came all the way down, pushing one another, screaming, cutting our skin on sharp rocks as we pulled ourselves out.

And then we were out, on our hands and knees on the ground, weeping, vomiting chestfuls of water and staring in horror at the heavy, unmoving cover floating flat on top of the water. And counting the children, ten, only *ten*. Ten children and me, eleven of us, *two missing*.

And then, and now the telling is almost over, the cover began to lift, on pulleys of rope from somewhere, lifting slowly until it was completely off the surface of the water, and underneath it, floating, two bloated bodies, dead, dark and light, drowned, blond Karen and black Susanna, dead, their bodies floating on top of the water.

They take us in bits and pieces, hurting and hurting, each time one or two of us, each time like pulling flesh from a body, hurting so but not quite enough to kill us all—

Miss Love won't be mad at me for taking the book because I have a good idea, and I have to write it down. I tried to tell it to Nadia but she was too sick to understand. And I'm going to tell everybody, but first I want to write it down here. I like to write it down because that way it's like telling myself too, and I also like to write it for Miss Love to see because I can tell it better writing it than saying it. That way I remember everything I have to say, instead of remembering some parts and forgetting the rest. I always forget parts when I get excited and talk fast.

I just had the idea last night. Well, I really dreamed it, but ideas are just like dreams to me, and dreams are just like ideas. And last night I dreamed I was in a movie. A lot of people were taking pictures of me sitting and standing and walking around, all ordinary things, and it was okay for a long time. But then they suddenly said, "Fall down!"

"What?" I said. "Fall down," they said again, "and play dead!"

And then it turned from a dream into a nightmare,

and they were monsters and after me. And then things began to happen that I knew right away were like here, and that gave me the idea.

When I ran up some stairs to get away from them, the steps jerked and I lost my balance and fell. I fell off the side and landed on pieces of glass and was cut and bleeding all over. That's just like here, except here nobody fell off yet. But I had to get up because they were still after me. So I got up and ran and ran, but I wasn't getting away because I couldn't breathe. There was a fire, with red licking flames and black, black smoke, and I was standing right in the middle of it! And that's just like the black smoke that came here and killed a whole room of children, but not me. Then the monsters in the dream were almost on top of me, but I couldn't move! I was stuck in the ground and sinking down, just like what happened to Lexi and Gail! And then they came up to me, and I could see they still had their cameras! Their teeth were clicking open and closed like shutters, their eyes were staring, and they raced at me, their faces taking pictures of me while their hands killed me—and then the ceiling came down and crushed me underneath it, and I couldn't get out.

Finally I woke up.

So this is my idea: we're all in a movie! Really! I'm almost sure of it. They're trying to make some kind of movie about children in danger, and they caught us and brought us here to be in it. They don't care if we're scared, that's just what they want! They want pictures of scared children! And they don't care how worried they make our mothers and fathers, they just want movies of us and don't care about anything else. And when they're finished they'll send us home and won't even say thank you.

And I don't believe anybody's dead, because I don't think they could do that. What I think is they just want us to *think* Donna and Mark and Steven and Gail and Susanna and all the other ones are dead, so we'll be even more scared. But they faked it every time, with dummies and tricks, and either they already sent all those kids home, or else they still have them here somewhere, where we can't see them, and they're taking movies of them, too, in different dangers than we're in, and especially afraid because they're away from Miss Love.

Anyway, that's my idea.

Greg

I just got the book from Greg. He stole it from Miss Love! I never thought he could steal anything. And I'm reading it soon, this whole book. Maybe there's stuff in it I don't know. I can just read it very fast, and I will.

And I can climb that fence. I can *still* climb it if I want to, even if it does have that shock on the top. It's like an electric chair up there! But I'm not scared of it, and I figured out a way I can still get over it. It's easy. I'm pretty sure it's only electric on the really top part, where the pointed wires all end and stick up. They have all the electric in them, it's not anywhere else. So I just have to be careful not to touch that part on the very top, and even though the whole fence tips a little inward up there

I still think I can do it. I just have to be sure that after I'm all the way up I don't do any holding on at all, and then just step right over the electric part and get on the outside and climb down. I know I can do it.

JEFFREY

June the 16th

Gregory and Jeffrey have both had this book. I cannot tell how much they have read, but perhaps only a little— I do not think they had it for very long, and they seem to have written so much in it that they could not have had much time left for

But I was wrong.

I had just gotten the book back from Jeffrey and had time to write only the very few sentences above, and no time at all to read what they had written, when I looked up to find them both standing before me.

"Did you read what I wrote, Miss Love?" Gregory said. "About the movie?"

I told him I had not, yet, because I had not had time to, and then I asked him why he had taken the book when he knew I wanted all the children to leave it alone, at least for the time being.

"You mean we really can't read it, Miss Love?" Jeffrey said. "I thought it was Nadia's."

"Why can't we read it, Miss Love? We want to know what you're saying!"

"Gregory, and Jeffrey, please listen," I said. "It is not

that I do not want you to read it. It is just that I do not
want you to read it right now."

"But when can we?"

"But why not, Miss Love?"

They spoke together. "Just not now, and because it
would be better not to. All right?"

"Well, but I did read it a little, Miss Love," Gregory
said. "And you wrote so much in it about Raymond. And
he's not even in our class!"

I smiled at him.

"And he says everybody who comes here dies! But I
don't believe him, and Jeffrey doesn't either. Right,
Jeffrey?"

"Yeah, he just thinks that because all the kids in his
class did. But it's not the same with us, because we stick
together, and we have you, Miss Love. Nobody else has a
teacher."

"And anyway, they can't really kill us," Gregory said.

And so I cannot keep this book from the children any
longer. Jeffrey and Gregory have read all I have written,
and will speak of it, so I cannot keep it from Nadia and
the others who will ask for it. But it is all right. They do
not believe Raymond. And perhaps he is wrong! Perhaps
it is not so!

"Jeffrey, and Gregory," I said, "I think you are right!
We will stick together, and we will surprise Raymond:
we are not going to die!"

"I know," Jeffrey said. "But anyway, what about him
and you?"

"Yes," said Gregory. "If you love him so much, what about us?"

"But children, that does not change anything! Raymond is very nice, that is all. He is my friend, and he will be yours too, if you will let him be. I want you to like him."

"But Miss Love, why don't you read what I wrote?" Gregory said, forgetting about Raymond.

"All right, Gregory," I said, "I will. I will read it right now."

"Okay," he said. And then I turned to the book, and they walked away.

And now I have read it. Jeffrey's writing and Gregory's. Jeffrey thinks he can still get over the fence. He is wrong, I will have to speak to him.

And Gregory thinks all this is make-believe. And no one is dead. And we are all going home.

iv

Some Lovely Place

I want to go
Someplace
Some far, lonely
Lovely someplace
No matter where
Someplace is
I don't care.

—BY ALIYSHA, age 10½

It's so dark. I'm all better now, but everything is just so dark. I was sick for a long time, with a terrible fever that wouldn't go away, until after a long time I started getting better. Then at first I couldn't see well and I was afraid, but Miss Love said she thought it was only because of the fever and little by little it would improve, and in a little while it did. Now it's almost all better: I can see everything, just not for too long at once yet. After I use my eyes for a while I have to rest them, or I get a terrible headache. But not being able to see too well at first isn't what I meant when I said it was so dark. That was different.

It's the air. Whenever they make us go outside now it's so black that day almost looks like night. Miss Love says it will pass, Raymond told her it happens every once in a while and then it goes away, so I guess it will. But it's still here now, and it's terrible. The air is full of soot that's just hanging there, all the way down to the ground, so there's no room left underneath it anymore, and there's so much of it that it fills every inch of the air until it's really almost black, not quite as dark as night but almost. All the daylight is locked off by the soot. And so much floats inside too, into our rooms. We can't see in it, and it hurts our throats and chests to breathe it but of course we have to breathe it to live, so we're coughing all the time. But at least it's not poisoned, since no one's died from it yet.

And all our moods are the same as the air, dark. There are only eleven of us left, ten children and Miss Love, and we never talk about leaving anymore, we try not to even think of it. And now I'm writing here again, but I didn't for such a long time—I was sick, but I didn't before that either. I was so unhappy I didn't want to do anything, we were all like that. Then Paul and Mark and Peter died and that made us stop acting like zombies, but we were terribly nervous and afraid of everything. Then I got sick, and now I'm better but the air is so bad. We don't feel like zombies again but we're unhappy all the time. But now I'm writing here, so I'm probably getting better.

I kept reading the book though, even after I stopped writing in it, just the way Miss Love says. Miss Love wrote so much while I was sick. And Greg did too, and even Jeffrey wrote a little, even though Miss Love took the book away for a while because she thought it upset us to read it. But now she gave it back, and I have a lot to write.

While I was so sick I kept waking up, just for a minute each time but many, many times. And sometimes Miss Love was there, but sometimes she wasn't. Sometimes she was outside the door with Raymond, talking. Or making love.

I heard them. They were trying to be quiet but I did. There are always noises you hear when people are making love, and you're supposed to be sleeping but you hear them and know they're doing it. Like moving sounds all in a line, and loud breathing and panting and other sounds like those. And I heard them. They make love, and Miss Love loves Raymond, and he loves her.

I was still sick when I first heard them and found out, and I didn't think about it very much. But now I'm better and I read the book, and I really know they love each other. She loves us too, but she loves Raymond, and I'm so worried about it because I don't know what will happen to us now because of it. Miss Love says it doesn't change anything, but it isn't as if she was just loving one extra child, that isn't how she loves him. She loves us, but she's *in love* with him, and being in love is different from just loving, especially from loving children. Being in love with Raymond might make Miss Love leave us. I don't mean go away, she wouldn't do that, and she couldn't, but look at our mothers, at home: they take care of us, cook our food and buy our clothes and don't let us go anywhere dangerous, but they don't spend time loving us. Miss Love says it's because they're too busy.

But not Miss Love. She's different. She always has time to love us, no matter what. But now I keep thinking she won't have love or time to spare for us anymore! And I'm afraid of that, I'm afraid it will happen and I don't want it to!

And I don't understand how Raymond can always be with Miss Love! Why do they let him? He isn't supposed to, but they must know about it and they don't do anything, so Miss Love keeps being with him instead of us!

I don't know what we would do without Miss Love. They're trying to kill us, she has to take care of us! Children keep dying, half of our class are dead!

I don't know what we'll do if Miss Love leaves us.

NADIA

My name is Joanne Novo and I am ten years old. I haven't written anything in this whole book.

Nadia is running this whole book. Miss Love writes in it too, but almost nobody else does. But now Nadia finally had to give me a turn because we're supposed to be best friends, though I'm not so sure of it. And Miss

Love came just when I was getting the book from Nadia and she was saying okay, Joanne, but just don't take long because I still have to tell about what happened with the black air. But then Miss Love said of course I should write in it, and Nadia knew she had to let any of us write in it who wanted to, even though she's still the one in charge of it, but I might just as well be the one to tell about how the blackness in the air finally went away. So I'll tell it.

Nadia already wrote about how terrible it was, just black all the time so it always seemed like night. Well, it lasted eight days, the same every day. And then yesterday we were all outside and all of a sudden we felt strange. We felt as though something funny was going on, and we looked and looked to see what it could be.

We were standing all in a line, holding hands. That's something we did all the time the black was here, but I guess now we won't do it anymore, holding hands whenever they made us go out in it so we wouldn't get lost or separated from the rest. The black made us afraid that would happen. So we were all standing there holding hands and looking and looking, when finally Nadia gasped, "Miss Love, look! Down by the ground!" And we looked and saw it, a line of clearness that was moving up off the ground, inch by inch, just like a curtain lifting on a stage when the show is about to start, because the black soot was rising up and leaving new, clear white air behind it, and it was so funny, a line like that moving up through the air! And then I saw something else.

"Miss Love!" I gasped too, and pointed at what I saw:

a whole army of the guards' black boots lined up in a row under the black air, as it rose up. Standing still in a line facing us and not moving.

And we couldn't move. We were standing right against the fence and couldn't, and the black air kept slowly rising, and with every inch it moved we saw more and more of the guards' bodies. And they were all black too, of course, so it looked as if the black air was going away leaving bits and streaks of itself behind, with the clean, fresh new air in between the streaks, and we saw boots, and ankles, and then legs, and then, a minute later, bodies—guards' bodies in their black uniforms, with their guns pointing at us and their fingers on the triggers.

Then up, up, up them the black air went, up their chests and necks and finally we were all standing there crying and holding hands and staring under the bottom of the black air right into the white monster faces of the guards, and they were staring at us, hard into our faces and eyes without looking away. One guard in front of every one of us, staring and staring, with their fingers on the triggers of their guns.

But then we weren't staring back anymore. Because we didn't stop! The black air that was still rising and rising up, over all the heads and into the sky, had hypnotized our eyes and we had to keep following it! Until at last we were looking straight up, with our heads all the way back, and we saw this: the sky, bright blue and not black anymore from where we were on the ground all the way until halfway up, and then a line right across the middle of the

sky, and above it the sky was gone! All the black was just
hanging there and staying there and not going up any
higher but not coming down again either. And now it's
the next day and it's still there, waiting and threatening
us, and I don't think it will ever go away again. And it
isn't just the color of black either. Even seeing it all the
way up there, where it is now, it's heavy and ugly and bad
and hating us, as if it wants to hurt us.

I got a little confused. Anyway, we were standing
there, and it finished going up, and then the spell was
broken and we all looked back down again, so scared and
afraid remembering the guards waiting there with their
guns pointing at us, and they weren't there! They were
gone!

We looked at Miss Love, but she was as mixed up as
we were. Our hands hurt from how hard we'd been
squeezing the ones we'd been holding on to the whole
time, and how hard they'd been squeezing us back. We
came back to our room, and Nadia didn't even write
about it, because she couldn't. No one did anything, we
were just too upset.

We thought they were going to shoot us all, but nobody even got hurt.

Nadia's waiting for the book back now.

I was resting while Joanne wrote that, and then she
was just giving me the book back because she was finished when something else happened.

At least all of us are all right. But we don't know where
Miss Love is! She was here before, but now this hap-

pened and we can't find her, and we need her, and everyone's so frightened! What happened is they brought some new children in and rushed them up the stairs. First we just heard them downstairs crying, and then the guns and shooting and stamping and rushing sounds, and soon falling noises with poor children screaming on the stairs and some running down the hall. They didn't come past our door though, and we don't know how many of them fell or died because we didn't dare leave our room to find out. We were too afraid. And it's later now but we're still afraid to, we're sure some of them died from the way it sounded.

We're pretty sure this is the first time new children have been brought here since we came, and I wonder what it means. Maybe they'll lose interest in us now and just leave us alone! Even if we still couldn't go home, it might not be too bad. Maybe we could even get Miss Love to teach us here! She loves to teach us! We could all pretend it was really only a school, and forget all about everything else. Like a school where you sleep over and don't go home.

I just looked and there's only a quarter of the space in this book left. What if I can't fit everything in?

NADIA

This is Kenneth again.

We're still here, and all I ever wrote in this book was about the motorcycles a long time ago, and nothing else. We never had to ride them again though, yet. But we're still here, and now many children are dead. And it's sad about them, but mostly everybody keeps thinking they miss them and everything but the next time something else happens is it going to be me? Or is it still going to be someone else and not me yet? I guess nobody cares as long as it's not them. No, they do care, but they forget about the ones who died as fast as they can because if you don't forget you feel too scared.

But Miss Love's not here and that's what everyone's upset about. Because where could she be? She wouldn't go away from us. So she must be hurt, or else she would be here. But we're afraid to go and look for her because those new children came, and a lot of them got killed, so we want to stay in here so we don't get killed too. And Nadia keeps saying Miss Love is all right and not hurt and she will be right back. She doesn't know that, but she keeps saying it anyway because she doesn't want us to go out of our room right now because it's too dangerous, so she says Miss Love is all right and will be right back, and we're all staying here and waiting.

My hair grew so long now my mother wouldn't know it was me anymore. And two of my teeth are out too. Nobody in our whole house would know. We have a whole apartment building with two apartments on every floor, and my family owns it, together with two other families. Only Chinese people live there. And all the children walk to school together in the morning with one family's grandmother, and come home all together at three o'clock too. But now they all go without me and don't know where I am. But I guess they forgot about me by now.

I don't want to write anymore.

KENNETH

Something else terrible happened now, something awful. We're so upset. This morning they brought those new children and we heard them screaming and crying, and now this.

And I heard it too. When it first began I pretended I didn't know what the others were talking about, but they soon knew I did. I just thought I should pretend I didn't, to try to calm them down the way Miss Love would, because Miss Love isn't here, she still isn't, and we don't know what to do.

We don't know where she is, all this morning we haven't seen her, and I'm so frightened. I'm trying not to be and I keep telling the others she'll be right back, but I am.

This is what happened: we all heard something, *inside our heads.* A strange voice. And we heard it all at the same time too, so it's not as if somebody was going crazy or something. If just one of us heard it we might have thought that, but we all did, so it was really there: first just a sound moving inside our heads, and we didn't know what it was, but then it began to sound like a voice, saying words. But we couldn't hear what the words were. We could hear the voice going up and down, up and down, the same way every time, but we couldn't tell what it was saying. Then the words got clearer and

154

louder, and we started being able to hear what they were, but just as we were about to, music began, right along with the words, so we still couldn't tell. And it was strange music too, like church music or funeral music. Just horns, long, low, slow blows through horns, right along with the words.

Everyone was whispering, looking around frowning and touching each other and rushing over to me saying where is Miss Love? Do you hear it? Do you hear it too? What is it? and then stopping to listen to it again and see if they could tell what the words were going to be, because you kept thinking you'd be able to understand them any minute. And all the time we were listening to it all *inside* us, while we stared around at each other, terrified because even though it was inside our heads and we all heard it there was no sound in the room, not any at all! Except for us running around whispering what is it? what is it? our room was completely silent, while inside the rooms of all of our heads there was the horn, W-a-a-a-a-a, W-a-a-a-a-a-a, W-a-a-a-a-a, and the voice, and the words we still couldn't hear well enough to understand.

And then we began to understand them.

And they went Waaaaaaaaaaaa-waaaaaaaaa guarrrrrrrrd *children* aaaaaaaaaa-waaaaaaaaaaa to the waaaaaaaaaa-waaaaaaaa *guardhouse* waaaaaaaaaaaa.

It was soft the first time we heard it, but then it changed. The music got louder, and we could hear the breath of the man who was blowing it and almost feel the wetness of his breath, and then the words came again, and again and again, and it wasn't soft anymore, *guard children waaaaaa-waaaaaaaaa to the* guardhouse, and the words were still low and moaned but the music kept getting louder inside our heads, until it was only the music that we could really hear. Except somehow we *could* still hear the words too, maybe coming through the music or maybe we just remembered them going with the music so well that even if it was only the music by then we thought the words were still coming, and so we still heard them. I don't know, but we did. And of course by then all the others knew I was hearing exactly the same thing they were, because just like them my hands were against my head and my ears as hard as I could get them to try to make the sounds stop, and my mouth was wide open and gasping for air because I couldn't breathe anymore and the noise was drowning me.

But finally, when we thought we were all deaf and drowned and it would never stop, it ended.

There wasn't a sound.

We were too shocked to say anything for a long time. Then we all started talking at once.

"What does it mean?"

"What was it?"

"Oh, where's Miss Love!"

"I want Miss Love!"

"But what was it!"

"Guard children to the guardhouse! They're calling for us! They want us to become guards!" Anthony shouted.

"Oh, no, that's disgusting!" cried Aliysha.

156

"They want us to leave our class and be against us?" Jeffrey said.

"Maybe they think we'll all come, and there'll be none of us left to be against!"

"All be guards?" cried Yvette.

"Oh, no! Remember what they *do*?" said Kenneth.

"What do they do? What do you mean what they do?" Jeffrey said, looking at the rest of us.

"Everybody knows, Jeffrey," I said, "you just don't know because you never read the book! But at least you could listen when we talk!"

"Listen!" he screamed. "And that stupid *book*! I read almost all that stupid asshole book! What do you think this is, school?"

"Don't you speak to me like that, Jeffrey! You're stupid! Everyone knows you're stupid, and you *didn't* read the book! You don't even belong in Miss Love's class!" I'm sorry I said that, but he shouldn't have talked to me like that.

"I never wanted to be in your stupid asshole class!" he screamed back at me. "If I wasn't in your stupid class I wouldn't be here, you asshole, Nadia! Who the shit wants to be in your class!"

"You shut up, Jeffrey!" Anthony shouted, "or I'll make you!"

Someone started to cry.

I looked at them. I had to think of what to say. We *can't* fight, we have to fight them! What would Miss Love say to make them stop?

But I didn't know. I decided to just talk to them very quietly, the way Miss Love does, so they'd have to stop to hear me. "Children," I said, very softly, "fighting is not the thing to do to help ourselves."

And it worked! They stopped for a second so they could hear me, and I went on before they could start yelling again, still as softly as before. "Jeffrey, I'm sorry I said you were stupid, and you should be sorry for what you said to me. But fighting is a terrible thing to do right now, and we mustn't do it. It's them we have to fight, not ourselves! We have to stop it so we can talk and figure out what to do."

And they really did stop! They were so surprised to hear me talking like Miss Love that they quieted down and listened to me! Jeffrey's face was so red with anger he looked like he was burning up, even though he's dark-skinned, because he's from—no, wait, he's not from anywhere, he's American, but his mother's white and his father's black, that's it. But he doesn't look like a regular mulatto kid, so you forget it all the time. He has smooth, soft black hair, a wide face, black eyes, and brown skin. Well, maybe his father's not Negro, but something else like Indian. I'm not sure. But anyway, through his brown skin his face was burning red, he was so angry. And Anthony, who's built the same as Jeffrey, big and strong, but looks just the opposite because of his blond hair and pale skin and light colored eyes, wasn't red with anger, he was white with anger, but with the spots of bright red on his nose and cheekbones that he gets when he really is.

But they both stopped yelling and looked at me, and then everyone else did too.

"Thank you everybody," I said. "And now no more fighting. Especially with Miss Love away for a little while we all have to try to help ourselves."

"But Nadia, where is Miss Love!" Lizabeth said.

"Yes, why isn't she here! Where could she be?" said Aliysha, starting to cry.

"Yes, Nadia, you keep saying she'll be right back, but something could have happened to her!" Kenneth said.

"But she will! She'll be right back, and we don't have to worry, I know it!"

"All right, Nadia, but what about what we heard?" Jackie cried.

"Wait, not yet," I said. "First Jeffrey doesn't know about the guards, and now there's no time for him to read the book." I turned to him. "Jeffrey, Greg and Kenneth and I snuck down to see the guards, off duty. At night. They have a big room, and it's filled with them smoking and drinking, taking dope and having sex!"

"Don't forget about the food, Nadia," said Kenneth.

"Yes," I said, "they have a lot of food. But they have sex, with each other, Jeffrey. They're homosexuals!"

"They're what?" Jeffrey said.

"You know, men and men. Together, having sex."

"Sucking on each other, and kissing," Kenneth said.

"Sucking on their . . ." Greg started, but then he didn't say it.

"Like candy, you said in the book, Nadia," Jackie said.

"You mean queers?" Jeffrey squeaked.

"It's disgusting!" Lizabeth said.

Then all of a sudden I thought of something. "Wait a minute!" I said. "I just remembered something! How could we be guards? How could they want us for guards? We're not grown up!"

"That's right!"

"And some of us are girls!" cried Lizabeth.

"That's right too, I never thought of that before! Now I don't understand at all!"

"It must be a trap, Nadia!" Yvette said.

"Yeah," shouted Jeffrey, "I bet they don't want us for guards at all, and it's just another way to try to kill us!"

"The doorknob!" Kenneth shouted. "Nadia, remember? Miss Love, in the book! She went down to try to get some medicine for you, and when she touched the doorknob to the guards' room it gave her a terrible shock that knocked her down!"

"And it wouldn't just knock us down, we're smaller than Miss Love!" Jackie cried. "It would kill us!"

"Just what they want!"

"But maybe not."

It was Anthony.

"What do you mean, maybe not?" I said.

"Oh, I don't know. Maybe it's not a trap, and they wouldn't use the doorknob. They might really want us to come, and have some way to just change everybody right into a grown-up man or something."

We thought about that. Then I remembered how Raymond told Miss Love that his classmates who became guards were changed, and he never even knew which ones they were. I told the others.

"But Nadia, do you really think they could do that?" said Aliysha.

"I don't," Lizabeth answered.

"I don't think so," I said, "but even if they could, you'd still be a guard! And have to . . ."

"Yeah, but at least you'd be alive," Anthony said, turning away.

Oh Miss Love, where are you?

I am here, Nadia.

And I know now this book belongs to the children, not to me. I will not use it much more. It will be Nadia's, and all the other children's. For nearly all of them have read it, they read it and go on. They are so brave and good. And what an amazing child Nadia is, trying to take care of all the other children by herself! I am so proud of her, of them all. Though I must speak with Anthony, he worries me. And Jeffrey's violence! But Nadia handled it so beautifully.

I did not hear what the children heard. But I am sure they did hear it, and perhaps I did not simply because I am not a child. But then, why am I here? I have thought so much about that! Did they mistake me for a child when they captured us, and bring me here by accident? I do not know. Because this is a place of children.

But Raymond said the ones who did not become guards died! All except him. Oh, Raymond, if anything happened to him, I do not know what I would do. How could I go on? Oh why is there no way out of here, is there really none? For all of us, the children and Raymond and me, for us all?

Only in dream. When Raymond loves me, then I escape from this place, I travel deep into the silence and sound of myself and find escape. And it is the same for him. Raymond's hands, when they touch me—I have never known feelings like these before.

But now I must do some things. I must try to forget Raymond for most of every day, and care for my children, and I must not go to Raymond's room with him again, oh I must deny myself that. I was not gone very long, but the children were so upset. But perhaps only very rarely—it is so wonderful to be by ourselves, to move, with a door between us and everything else, oh Raymond, I love you.

The book! I have been writing all this, and the children will read it! I thought I was talking to myself only, speaking in my mind—

I cannot destroy this book! I heard myself deciding that that was what must be done. But I must not, I cannot do it to the children! They depend on it so, for some reason, it is their classroom, their home. They feel safer with it, within it, I will never take it from them again. I must discipline myself not to write in it again, or at least not of Raymond and myself. Not again. Oh, I know:

Dear Children,
I am writing this letter to you to tell you something that you already know very well, but may perhaps

forget. And you may not do so. No matter what happens, you may not forget this: I love you, and I am proud of you all. If you do forget, read this and remember again: I love you. Have I said it already? Then it will make you smile! Listen to Nadia if ever I am not right here, and remember to read this again and again, so you will know. Have I said it before? I love you!

MISS LOVE

No. Oh, that is fine, but I must speak of it to the children myself too, so they can see my face and smile and hear my voice as I tell them, and I can touch them, here and there, and they touch me, and it will be better. And it will still be here in the book for them to read again whenever they need to, and as they read it they will think of me saying it to them too, and that will be good.

Miss Love did.

We fell asleep from exhaustion and she came and got the book, and no one even knew it. When she came back we were just waking up, but of course the minute we saw her we jumped up and ran to her, all talking at once.

"No, children, wait," she said, smiling at us. "Tell me everything in just a minute." Then she turned to me.

"Nadia, here is the book."

"Oh, thank you Miss Love, I . . ."

"No, Nadia, wait. First I want to tell everyone something."

She looked around at all of us, and then said, "It is just

this very important thing, children: I love you. You are a wonderful, wonderful class. I have read everything in the book, and you are all brave, good children and I am so pleased with you. And I love you all."

And she sat down and gathered us close around her, and hugged us tight while she told us over and over how much she loved us, and how she was so pleased with us she couldn't be happier. Her voice was so sweet and soft it made everyone feel wonderful.

Then she looked at Jeffrey and said she was so proud he'd been able to control himself, and to Anthony she said, "We will have to talk soon, Anthony, all right?" And she kept saying she loved us and we would be all right. "Oh, and I love the idea of our having our school here, Nadia," she said. "We will talk about that soon too."

And then she smiled and got up and walked to the door.

"Oh no, Miss Love where are you going? Where were you?" cried Aliysha, standing up and starting after her.

"No, don't go, Miss Love! You have to stay with us!" Lizabeth echoed her.

But Miss Love only looked strange, and smiled again in a funny way and said, "I will be back right away, children, do not be so silly!" And she left.

We stood staring after her.

"I bet she was with Raymond," Joanne said. "And she's going there again." Aliysha started to cry, and Lizabeth did too.

"Raymond! The worst thing in this whole place is Raymond!" Anthony said.

"Yes, he is!" Joanne cried. "Miss Love would never leave us like that, she wouldn't, so he must be *making* her do it! How can he do that! I hate him!" She started crying too, and everyone looked so miserable I didn't know what was going to happen. I went in front of them all.

"Miss Love is right!" I said. "She said you were being silly and you are! Of course she'll be back soon! Stop crying!" And after a minute they did.

"Okay, Nadia," Aliysha said.

"Yes," said Yvette, "she said she would. And at least we know she's all right now."

I smiled at them. "Now, when did our food come last?" I said. I was trying to change the subject.

"None came since this morning, Nadia, and it's so late already," Kenneth answered.

"Oh well, it will be here soon," I said. "Now when it comes we have to share it out exactly, but somebody else has to do it: Joanne. Everybody listen to Joanne, while I go and write." And I went to write all this down.

It must really be late now. But I don't care, I just don't feel like sleeping yet.

I'm writing very small now, but there's not much room left in the book at all.

The food just came. I'm eating now—saltines, a carrot with its peel still on, and a dark-brown apple, I mean I'm pretty sure it's an apple. It's the middle of the night, and we're all still up eating. I guess no one feels like sleeping, we're just too upset about Miss Love. She still hasn't come back, and we want to stay awake to talk to each other. I mean we know she loves us the way she said, but why does she have to go away from us? I know she wouldn't if she could help it, but she has to be here! We need her. We wouldn't mind that much if Raymond was here too, if he had to be, but he can't keep Miss Love somewhere away from us! And anyway, how can he make her do it, go away from us to be with him? I can't understand it, he must have some secret power to be able to do it. It's not just because she loves him, she could love him and still stay with us, but he makes her leave us all alone, and that's bad. That's as bad as the quicksand or cars or the guards. And Raymond must know that, and he still does it, so he's as bad as the guards! We need her more than he does! Maybe he's really a secret guard!

And it's so terrible, because without Miss Love we're just like orphans. All alone, with no one to tuck us in and kiss us goodnight. That's what I always used to say to my mother when she said I didn't need to be tucked in anymore because I was too big, I told her I felt like a child with no parents if she didn't. I didn't know the right word then, because I was much younger, I think about six. But it was orphan, I felt like an orphan, and I remember how it felt, and when Miss Love smiled just before and went out the door that way, it felt almost the same. We know she loves us, but we're all alone and we're so lonely for her.

Now I'm finished eating, and I still don't feel like going to sleep.

Just then Jackie came racing in, whispering loudly, "Come on, everybody come with me!"

"What? Where are we going? What's going on?" we asked all at once.

"*Shhhhhh!*" she hissed. "Just come, and be quiet, act like nothing's up."

So we all followed her, down the stairs and outside. We were very nervous, because we hate to go outside, but she wasn't. And she had been out all by herself, and in the *back* too, where we're never supposed to go, because that's where it is and she found it. We were all afraid when we saw we were going in the back. But Jackie wasn't. I bet she's the least afraid of all of us here.

When she showed us what she found we were so excited we couldn't keep quiet, and we had to keep saying "Shhhh!" to each other every minute.

It's a tunnel!

"Jackie! Did you go down it?" we cried.

"An escape tunnel!"

"Shhhhh!"

"I went down it for a long way," she whispered, "but then I didn't want to go any more without all of you, in case something happened to keep me from turning around and coming back. You know, like if the tunnel gets very narrow or something, like in the movies, and the way they say some tunnels get narrow after a while. Then I would just have disappeared and never come back, and you wouldn't have known what happened to me. But it's a real tunnel, and it goes on and on, and I think it goes straight to the fence! It'll go underneath it and out of here!"

"Yeah!"

"Shhhhh!"

"But what about the electric?" Kenneth said.

"What?"

"You know, the shock on the top of the fence. Do you think they do it underneath the ground too, and we'll crawl and crawl through the tunnel and when we get to the part that's underneath the fence we'll all get electrocuted?"

We thought about that.

"No," said Jackie, finally. But everyone looked at me.

"No, we won't, Nadia," Jackie said again. "I'm sure we won't."

"No, I don't think so either," I said. "Let's try it! I'll go first, very, very carefully, just an inch at a time, and we'll see."

"No, not you, Nadia, I'll go first!" Jackie shouted. "Me!"

"Shhhhh!"

I looked at her.

"Okay," I said. "You go first, I don't care. But you won't get hurt, I'm sure the electric is only on the outside. I don't think they could get it underneath the ground."

"Me neither," Jackie said.

"Okay," said Kenneth, "then me neither. I only

thought I should say it in case no one else remembered it."

The tunnel is in the back, behind the hotel, where we almost never go, and the entrance to it is hidden behind some big rocks. That's why we never saw it before.

"Well come on, let's go!" Jackie said.

I looked at her. "Now?"

"Yes, now!"

"But we can't! Miss Love!"

"Miss Love!" Jackie cried. She looked terribly shocked, at herself. "Oh, how could I forget Miss Love? Nadia, I would never want to leave Miss Love behind! I don't want to go without her!"

"I know, Jackie, it's okay," I said. "Let's go back right now and find her, and then we'll go! Right, everybody?"

"And Miss Love will go first! She'll lead us!" said Kenneth.

"No, she won't, Kenneth! I won't let her!" Jackie said. "Not because I found the tunnel and it's my idea or anything, because of the electricity! In case it is there after all. Miss Love can't go first because then she'd get hurt instead of me even though it would be my fault. I have to go first!"

"Okay, Jackie," I said, and then everybody said okay too, Kenneth last.

And we went back. All the way Jackie kept saying, "I love Miss Love, I would never want to go anywhere without her," and we kept telling her it was all right until finally she felt better, and then we were back.

But maybe I shouldn't have written it all down about

the tunnel! What if the guards get the book and find out, then we couldn't escape! I'll have to keep the book in my hands every minute from now on, and never put it down anywhere, until we escape.

The guard call came again.

We got back to our room, and I wrote about the tunnel while Jackie went to try and find Raymond's room, where we thought Miss Love would be, and all of a sudden it started again.

It was inside our heads exactly like the first time. We were staring at each other in the outside silence out of the terrible sounds that were inside us, and it was the same: first just the voice, then the music too, Aaaaaaaaaaa, Aaaaaaaaa, Waaaaaaaaaa, Waaaaaaaaaa, and the breath, with Waaaaaaaaaahhhh Waaaaaaaaahhhh Waaaaaaaa-ahhhh for a long time, and then the voice again, in be-tween the horn blows, with the sound of the words com-ing but not the words themselves yet, and then at last the words beginning and the sound growing louder and louder just like before waaaaaaaaa waaaaaaaaaaa guard waaaaaaaah children aaaaaaah waaaaaaaaah to the waaaaa-aaaaa waaaaaaaa guard aaaaaaaaaaaa waaaaaaaaaaa waaaaa-aaaaaaaa children to the guard waaaaaaaaaa house guard children waaaaaaaa waaaaaaaaa to the guard waaaaaaaaahhh house waaaaaaaaAAAAHHHH WAAAAAAA WAAAA-AAAA it went, on and on and getting louder and louder until we were covering our ears and holding our heads, WAAAAAAAAA WAAAAAAAAA GUARRRRRRR-RRD CHILDRENNNNNNNN TO THE GUAAAAA-

'AAARRRRD WAAAAAAAA HOUSE WAAAAAAA-
AAA, looking at each other, and it went on.

And another thing started, that wasn't there before.

All at once we couldn't move. The sounds got louder
than ever before, and suddenly we couldn't move at all.
We were stiff and twisted up, the noise was twisting us
and cutting us like knives. All of us. Except one. Anthony. He started to move.

As we watched, through the pain of the noise that was
twisting us so tight that we couldn't move an inch, we
saw Anthony get up. His hands weren't pressing his head
and ears like the rest of us. He got up, moving like a zombie. They were inside his mind and making him move.
Only him, no one else. And he moved like a zombie
through us, over to the door and out to the stairs. We
didn't see where he went because we couldn't move. But
we knew!

And we haven't seen him again. It's over and he's gone.

I think and think about him, and where he is now. I
just can't stop thinking about it. And why didn't any
others of us move? If they could get inside Anthony's
brain and make him go to them, then how come not the
rest of us too? Anthony's very smart. It isn't as if he was
stupid and couldn't fight them back. I have two ideas.
The first is that he really wanted to go, and that's how
they could get only him to do it. And the second is
that *they* wanted *him*, the way Raymond said in the book
they pick the ones they want, and only take them, and they
wanted Anthony and talked to him differently than
the rest of us. Instead of just saying GUARD CHIL-

DREN TO THE GUARDHOUSE WAAAA-WAAAA maybe they told him all about cake, and candy, and that taking dope and having sex with them was fun, and things like that.

But anyway, he's gone.

I keep wondering if we'll ever see him again, and what he'll look like if we ever do. How can they make him grow up all at once like that? Will it hurt him if they do? At least they don't have to change him from a girl to a boy! I can't stop thinking about it. Oh, if only he hadn't! We're all going to escape now! But will he look so different grown up that if we see him we won't even know it's him? Will he hit us and shoot at us and we won't even know it's him doing it? But maybe he won't know it's us anymore! Because he wouldn't hurt us! But maybe he wouldn't even know it was us.

But we're going to escape! I know the tunnel will work. Poor Anthony, even if he would have known it was us, and couldn't have talked to us but would never have hurt us, now he'll never even see us again. I feel so sorry for him. They made him go, and he could have gone home!

But he's gone.

I'm writing this all by myself in the other room, away from everyone else because I have to think about everything.

Jackie hasn't come back yet! I don't know if something happened to her or she just can't find Miss Love. But what if she can't, what will we do? We have to leave, but we can't without Miss Love! I don't know what to do.

172

I was still by myself in the other room, and Jeffrey came and found me.

"I'm leaving, Nadia," he said. "Right now, and I came to get the book. That's what it's for, right?"

"What do you mean, Jeffrey?" I whispered. "We're all leaving. We have to wait for Miss Love, but as soon as she gets here we're going. And I'll carry the book."

"No, I'm not coming with you. I'm going by myself, right now."

"Through the tunnel, by yourself? You can't!"

"I'm not, I'm going over the fence."

"The fence!"

"Well I'm not going through that tunnel! I know how to climb the fence, and I'm not going through any tunnels! All the rest of you can if you want but I hate tunnels, rats are in tunnels! And I *know* I can get over the fence."

"But what about the electricity, Jeffrey!"

"I can still do it. I figured it all out."

"How can you do it? You'll be electrocuted! I know what you said in the book, but . . ."

"No, Nadia, I *won't!* Now shut up! I'll climb up the fence, that's all, and when I get to the top I'll just balance for one second so I can swing my leg over without touching anything, and then my other leg, and down the other side and I'll be out. It's only electric on the very top!"

"But how do you know for sure?"

"I checked! I threw things at the fence, and there weren't any sparks at all."

"Only at the top?"

"Well, I couldn't reach the top. I couldn't throw high enough."

"But that doesn't . . ."

"It still proves it! Because there weren't any sparks at all!"

"But anyway, Jeffrey, even if it's only electric at the very top, how do you know for sure you can balance long enough up there to get over it without falling, or even just *touching!* All you'd have to do is touch it! And you'll have to turn around and everything!"

"I know, but I can do it. I'm good at things like that."

"But why are you scared of the tunnel, if you're not scared of going over the fence? I'd be much more scared of going over that fence. You're crazy to do it!"

"And you're crazy to go through that stupid tunnel!"

"Shhhhh! I'm not fighting! We don't want the guards to know about any tunnels or fences, so shhhh!"

"The guards never come up here!"

"Yes they do sometimes, they send guards up here all the time, to check on what's going on and everything, and you know it!"

"*Okay!* But do you want me to take the book over the fence or not?"

"But how could you even hold it? You need your hands to balance and to climb."

"I could put it under my shirt."

"No, I have to keep it. I'll take it through the tunnel. Anyway I still have to write more in it before we go, if I have time."

174

"You mean about me! You have to write all about me climbing over the fence!"

"Well . . ."

"Well I don't care, go ahead. Say Jeffrey escaped over the fence tonight, and he's going to send the cops. That's good. I bet I'm not anywhere else in that book anyway, except where I wrote myself."

"Oh yes you are, Jeffrey. Why didn't you ever read it? You should have."

"I did read a lot of it. Anyway, goodbye, Nadia."

"Goodbye, Jeffrey. No, wait! What about Miss Love? Aren't you going to say goodbye to her?"

"I want to, but I can't! She'd never let me do it, and I'm not staying here! And I don't want to have to go after she tells me not to. Anyway, how do I know how long it'll take Jackie to find her? It's so late already, it might get to be morning, and I have to do it when it's dark. And I'm not going tomorrow, I'm going now. So you'll just have to tell Miss Love goodbye for me. And tell her I will send the cops to raid this place as soon as I'm out, the way I said, so if the tunnel doesn't work, don't worry."

"Okay, Jeffrey. Goodbye."

And we shook hands, and he left.

And about ten minutes later a terrible, terrible frightening noise came from outside. I forgot all about being afraid to and ran down the stairs, and the other children saw and followed me, though they didn't know about Jeffrey. And then we were down, and when we opened the door we saw, on the fence, off to the side and all the way up, so high, a big bright place where something was burning so hard it was bright white fire instead of red. We watched it burn for a minute, and then it slowly got darker and darker until we couldn't see it anymore. The other children were looking too but didn't understand, and then they saw my shocked face, and I had to tell them it was Jeffrey.

So here I am writing about Jeffrey climbing over the fence, but not the way he said. Poor Jeffrey.

Wait: while we stood there, it began to get light. Day was beginning, and we knew we'd have to wait until dark again to escape.

NADIA

July 10th

We are leaving this place—the children, Raymond, and I. Perhaps we are. Jackie has discovered a tunnel which seems to lead underneath the fence. It is afternoon now, and we are waiting only for the dark to come again. The children found the tunnel yesterday, last night, but we could not leave at once because the night came to an end before all was ready—before they found me.

Anthony went to the guards yesterday, and Jeffrey died trying to climb over the fence. I do not know how I can continue writing these things. Tell me, Raymond. I had meant to speak to Anthony, but did not do so in time. I went back to Raymond's room instead, although I said I would not, I must stay with the children. And then I could not stop myself, Raymond was waiting there, smil-

176

ing and talking and holding me when I came. I do not know how I could leave the children again. And then I intended to stay only for a few moments and return to the children, and I could not leave.

But although I can never really know, I do not think that I could have stopped Anthony, or Jeffrey. Perhaps I am only comforting myself with this. But truly the evil of this place is so terrible. It is inhuman, and I am human, only that, no more. My hand moves across this page without my will, once it begins I cannot stop it. I only want everything to be over, though what that may mean I do not know. I do not know. How can I believe we may escape from here? But Raymond is coming too, of course he is. He would never let me leave him.

Raymond has been here for so long, and yet he had never seen the tunnel. But he believes it may be real, and so I do too. He thinks he may never have seen it only because he never looked, because he never believed there was any slightest possibility or hope of escape from here. And then, when Jackie found us and told us, he stole out and saw it, and now he is excited and believes in it, and perhaps it is so, we may escape. Raymond. He thinks we may.

There are ten of us going: Raymond, Nadia, Gregory, Kenneth, Jackie, Lizabeth, Aliysha, Joanne, Yvette, and I. Ten children are dead. One has gone to the guards, and will be our enemy now, if we do not escape, Anthony, I cannot believe it. And Mark is dead, and Lexi, Steven, Gail, poor Susanna, poor Karen, Peter, Donna, Paul, and now Jeffrey, poor Jeffrey, oh why would he not wait?

177

Why would he not go through the tunnel with us? He has been so good all this time; now he too is dead. Nadia says he was afraid of the tunnel, he was afraid of tunnels, of rats. And so he burned up on the fence, instead. My children, oh may it stop now, may no more die! Raymond, if I did not have you I too would be dead, for how could I stand it. Raymond. We are going to try it. Perhaps it will work.

It took Jackie a long, long time to find us, lost in the frightening corridors of this place, coming on blank hallways again and again, opening doors onto nothing and wandering back and forth as if in a maze. She told us of it afterwards, when she finally found us. And she told us of the tunnel, and Raymond listened, doubted, listened again, I watched his eyes grow bright, and then he left us and stole out to see, so excited, and we waited. And when he returned he came to me, and with Jackie standing beside us, said, "We will try it. I think it's real, we're going out. I love you. We are going out together."

Miss Love is back! It just took Jackie a long time to find her, but now she's here and she's not going away again, she promised, and we're just waiting for night. If only nothing else happens before we can go. But Miss Love is right here and we're so happy, excited and happy. And Raymond too, of course, but we're leaving! We're all ready, and just waiting for night.

Here's Greg. He wants to write something. So I'm giving him the book now. I told him to stay right here with it, and be careful not to put it down anywhere because I wrote in it about the tunnel. And I hope he doesn't take up too much space, but it doesn't really matter because I probably won't have to write anything else and then we're escaping. This book is going to turn out to be just the right size.

NADIA

This is Greg again. Now I know it's true they're making movies of us, and no one will listen! Miss Love won't, and I even told Raymond just now, and all he did was smile at me. He didn't laugh, but he smiled. And Miss Love read it in the book and didn't say anything, I asked her and she didn't! So she doesn't believe it either. So before we try to escape through the tunnel I have to write it down a little bit more.

Miss Love, it *is* a movie! They have cameras all over, they're just hidden is all. There's probably one right this minute, taking pictures of us sitting here and me writing this! And they probably know all about the tunnel too. If they don't, maybe we'll really get out, but they probably do and then they'll just take pictures of us trying to escape and thinking we're going to escape and then not escaping. I would rather we did escape and go home right now, to show them they can't just capture children and keep them prisoners until they're finished with them, but then what about all the kids we'd be leaving behind? Mark and everybody, because maybe then they'd be so mad they really would kill them and just not care what happened to them afterwards because of it.

And Jeffrey. I saw that. That was a bunch of rags they

burned up there on top of the fence, and they burned it so they could take pictures of us watching and Nadia telling us it was Jeffrey and everyone being so scared and me just watching the bunch of rags burning up and knowing all along it was rags, and now Jeffrey is with all the other kids we're supposed to think are dead, which is maybe already home, with their mothers and fathers. I wish it was me, I mean I wish I was one of them and could be home. But I just thought about it and I decided actually they're probably not home because if they let them go home as soon as they got there they'd tell their mothers and fathers and the police and everyone about this place and them making us stay here so they can take pictures of children who are scared all the time, except we're not scared *all* the time and especially I'm not because I happen to know it's just a movie and nobody's really dead. But then the police would come, and they haven't, so I guess I don't really wish I was one of them after all because that means they aren't home, they're here somewhere and I don't know where and I do know what it's like here where I am, with Nadia and Kenneth and Joanne and Miss Love and everybody, and it's terrible but not that bad and I don't know where they're keeping the others or what it's like there is that noise again. Starting up and music sounds in my ears and everyone else's too because all looking around now it's getting louder again and sounds like always like the other times the terrible music terrible words and Anthony answered and went except really to the others because the guards are all actors, real ones though and not like us but Anthony sure isn't with them because he's only a boy so he's with the others now and now they have all the pictures they want of somebody, Anthony I mean, obeying them and being scared stiff like a zombie the voices *GUARD CHIL-DREN WAAAAA TO THE GUARDHOUSE WAAAA WAAAAA* and going to them they wanted *WAAAAA WAAAAA GUARD CHILDREN AAAA WAAAA WAAAA WAAA* and they got him *GUARD WAAAA WAAAA WAAAAAAAA*

It's over again. This time they got Joanne. Joanne
And this time Miss Love heard it too. She never did before, but the other times she wasn't in the room with us, and Jackie didn't hear it when she wasn't in the room either. But now Miss Love was here, and she heard it and Raymond did too, and they were paralyzed by the sound, just like us, and had to watch someone else, Joanne, the second one, get up and go to them. But I know Joanne didn't want to, because we talked all about Anthony and how terrible it was, and because she was my best friend and I know. So they must have told her different things to make her go, I know it. And this time it was even louder, it couldn't be but it was. We almost didn't see Joanne get up and go, we were twisted up so tight from the terrible, horrible, terrible noise, *WAAAAAAAAAAA WAAAAAAAAAAAAWAAAAAAAAAAAAAAA*

And Joanne got up straight, and stiff, not moving her body at all but only her legs, and walked out, moving just like a zombie. And when the noise stopped, and we could all move, Raymond suddenly jumped up and ran out the door too, and we heard him running down the stairs. After Joanne, it turned out later, to try and stop her, but he couldn't, she was gone. But Miss Love thought he was trying to join the guards too, and started crying and running after him. We held her and wouldn't let her go, and she cried and fought us, trying to follow him. Then Raymond came back, and we let her go. She ran to him sobbing, and when he looked at us we were frightened because he looked ready to kill us. He thought we had hurt her. But we told him what happened and then he just looked at Miss Love, saying "Oh, darling, no, I would never leave you, no, honey, no, nothing could make me."

But she kept on crying in his arms and couldn't stop. She crept closer and closer against him as if she wanted to make herself small enough to hide against him, and he wrapped his arms all the way around her, whispering, until finally she felt a little better. Then she looked around at us all, and said, with her face like a child's and her voice just like a child's, "I am sorry, everyone. All of you, children . . ." and then stopped because her eyes filled up again and she only said, "Joanne."

So I did have to write something else before we escaped.

And Joanne is gone.

And Greg is acting so funny. I just read it! What he wrote! I know he said almost the same thing before, all the way back in the book, while I was sick, but somehow it didn't sound as crazy that time as it does now. And he still thinks all the dead children are alive! And after Miss

Love stopped crying, finally, and then remembered Joanne was gone and started again, he went close to her
and touched her arm and said, "Don't cry, Miss Love,
Joanne's all right. Anyway, the movie will be over soon.
It has to be!" Then he laughed as though he said something so funny, and finally stopped, but just for a second,
to say, "They don't have so many of us left to go!"

Miss Love started shaking all over again when he said
that. But she got hold of herself quickly, and just put her
arms around him and didn't say anything.

So: I'll have to be ready to take care of Greg, in case he
can't take care of himself soon. And I think we have to
take care of Miss Love a little bit too. She looks so
weak.

But Raymond will do that, and I'll do Greg.

We worried a lot about whether Anthony or Joanne
would tell the guards about the escape, since they were
guards themselves now and might. But we decided to go
ahead anyway and just hope they hadn't. We were very
nervous though, because of that and also because of
Jeffrey trying to escape last night and getting killed. But
nothing could stop us, and as soon as it was dark Jackie
led us to the tunnel again.

Yvette was right behind Jackie. Then came Lizabeth,
Aliysha, Kenneth, Greg, me, Miss Love, and Raymond,
the nine of us that were left. I was near the back because
I wanted to be near Greg and Miss Love. And Miss Love
didn't say Jackie couldn't be the leader. I was sure she
would, but when she saw Jackie go in front and started to

say something, Raymond said yes, Jackie would be first, and she had to stay in the back with him. So that's how we stayed, and we got to the tunnel safely, walking single-file except for Miss Love and Raymond. He wouldn't let Miss Love away from him at all, so they were side by side at the end of the line.

Then we got there, and did what we'd already decided: went right in, not stopping for even a second outside, so there'd be the least chance of all of the guards seeing us. And then we were inside the tunnel. We stayed in single-file, with Raymond behind Miss Love now because they didn't fit side by side anymore. And we started walking.

It was very quiet, and we had no candles or matches or anything so it was dark almost from the beginning. And soon we were crawling: the tunnel did get low and narrow, just the way Jackie thought, and even Yvette, the shortest one of us all, couldn't stand up anymore. So we crawled along. I was very frightened, and so was everyone else, you could tell. And it was hard to breathe, the air was bad and it smelled terrible. But we kept going, and going and going. Our hands and knees were bleeding, and the tunnel just kept getting narrower. We thought it must really be deep, because we'd been in it so long and the air was so bad and everything, and we were sure we must be past the fence by then too, and with no shock. But it just kept going.

And then all at once it seemed to start slowly sloping *upwards*. We were sure it was. But it was terribly narrow too, and we were starting to be afraid we might have to give up and go back, because it was so narrow we almost couldn't move along it at all anymore, when it suddenly turned a corner and got wide. Really pretty wide, and high, too.

And then we could stand again. We stood up, smiled at each other—and realized that we could see each other, we could see! Very dimly, but we could see, and that meant that light, moonlight or starlight, was coming into the tunnel from somewhere, and we must be near the end! We were going to make it!

We started walking again. In the beginning we still went pretty slowly, but then the air got better and we could breathe easier, and it got even lighter, and we started moving faster and faster and then Jackie, way up in front, gave a scream and a laugh and began to run, grabbing Yvette's hand, with Yvette laughing and running right beside her! And we started running too, but pretty far behind them because they'd surprised us and had a good start on us, and as we ran we heard them ahead of us running too, talking and laughing and excited, and then suddenly came just Yvette's scream, not of laughter, and nothing from Jackie at all.

"Stop!" Miss Love cried, "Something is wrong!"

And we stopped. Miss Love and Raymond came up past us, it was wide enough then and there was enough room. "Wait here, children, and do not move," Miss Love said, but I crept behind them and the others followed me, and the light grew even brighter. But we heard nothing else from Jackie and nothing from Yvette. And then Miss Love and Raymond stopped. And we stopped behind them.

We were at the end of the tunnel.

And we were high, high up on a cliffside, though we'd never seen any cliff or mountain from our prison, but we were up on a cliff and the tunnel ended suddenly with a big, wide doorway and black sky and bright starlight pouring through it.

And Jackie and Yvette were gone.

Miss Love wouldn't let us lean out and look down. But she said she must and she did, with her arms stretched behind her and Raymond holding them so tightly she had marks on them afterwards, and her face, when she turned back, was just empty. There was nothing in her face. Her eyes didn't move, and her mouth didn't move. Then Raymond picked her up and started back through the tunnel carrying her, and we followed him, and we went on that way until the tunnel was low and narrow again. And then he put her down, and she crawled right behind him and we crawled right behind her until we were back near the beginning, and the tunnel got higher and wider again at last, and then we all stood up and walked, Raymond in the front, his hand behind him holding Miss Love's hand, until we got to the end and followed them out, and back to the hotel, and in the door and up the stairs to our room.

And when we got back Raymond took Miss Love to his room, and Greg and Kenneth and Lizabeth and Aliysha and I came in our room, and I wrote all this. And that's all there is to tell, except that just after I finished writing Kenneth and Lizabeth and Aliysha came over to me miserably and said, "What do we do now, Nadia?" And I said, "We do not do anything, children. We just live here, and that is all. But we are used to it now. It will not be so bad." I smiled at them, and they said yes, they were used to it.

But Greg was quiet, sitting by himself all the way across the room. "Gregory, what about you?" I said. "You must come and talk to us."

"In a minute," he said, but very strangely, hardly moving his lips at all and holding very still, so it sounded funny. "The film's running now. I don't want to move or they'll make me start all over."

And he just sat there.

I turned to Lizabeth and Aliysha and Kenneth. "I am afraid we must care for Gregory now, children," I said. "We will have to see that he eats and drinks enough, and moves from time to time, or he will become ill. But I cannot do it alone, you must all help me."

"But Nadia," Aliysha began to cry, "why won't Miss Love stay with us? I want her, why won't she?"

"She is with us, Aliysha," I said, very softly. "For now, I will be Miss Love. And you know she would be so ashamed of you if she heard that you were acting in a silly way. Miss Love loves us more than anything, she says so in the book many times, remember? But children do not go everywhere with grownups, you know that, Aliysha. And Miss Love is with Raymond right now. But she loves us all, and will always be here with us."

"But won't we ever see her, Nadia?" said Kenneth.

I smiled at him, but did not say anything.

"But Nadia, is Miss Love just like married to Raymond now?" asked Lizabeth.

"Well, not really, since they could not have a wedding or anything here. But yes, they are just the same as married, only without the wedding."

"Oh," they all said.

"But I will take care of you. I will be Miss Love, and take care of you, children, I promise that I will. But now, it is very late, and we must sleep."

"Yes," they said. Then Kenneth moved away, and Lizabeth and Aliysha did too, and they all lay down, and Gregory sat still.

July 25th

I saw Miss Love today, though she did not see me. I left the children alone, for the first time, with Kenneth in charge. He is very responsible, and I depend on him. I do not know what I would do without him.

I went to find Miss Love and Raymond's room, to see how Miss Love was. And I found it, but their door was almost closed. I could just see in though, and I could hear perfectly well. I did not eavesdrop. But standing outside their door I heard them speaking, and since Miss Love was telling Raymond of our picnic in the park, the day we were captured and brought here, I thought I should write it down, on almost the last page of this book, because it is about us.

She told him that the pollution that day was the worst it had ever been in The City, as bad as anything here, and how we had all gone to shelter in the little house where they captured us. And then:

Miss Love: And now I know, we should have gone right back. We should not have looked for a way to stay out for our picnic, Raymond, we should have turned around and gone right back to school, at once. How could I have kept the children out in that terrible air? And how could I have taken them inside a house I had never seen before? Oh, Raymond.

Raymond: It's all right. You didn't know.

Miss Love: I know, but I keep thinking about it, I cannot stop.

Raymond: Well, just don't. Think about me instead.

Miss Love: Oh, I do, I do all the time. But Raymond, I keep thinking about the picnic too, I cannot help it. I think, perhaps the soot is still coming down. Perhaps the sun is still shining somewhere above it, but we cannot see it, because it is not getting through. And perhaps we are still on the grass, in the black air, at the park, our sandwiches gray and gritty on our laps, as at the sea but with soot and not sand, and the pollution is still raining and raining and raining and raining down. And we did not get out.

Wait, I must stop for a moment. Otherwise I might fill the rest of the book with Miss Love and Raymond and their talk, and I want to say one or two more things first. Then in whatever space is left I will try to write the

189

rest of what they said, and that will be the end of the book.

First of all, Gregory: he is a little better. He is still very depressed and unhappy, and he dreams all night long, every night, but at least he does not just sit still all the time any longer, never moving, almost never speaking, because "the film is running." Some of the time still, but not all. Now he moves a little, and he is beginning to talk more too. Kenneth stays with him a great deal, and tries to help him.

But except for Gregory, who I am sure will be better soon, we are all fine. Lizabeth and Aliysha do not cry any more. They are being so good. And it is more than two weeks now since we tried to escape and Jackie and Yvette died, and nothing else has happened. And here is what I think: *nothing else is going to happen.* They are finished with us. We do not have the guard calls any more, so they do not want any others of us for the guards. There have been no new dangers, only the old ones, and of those we are very careful. The guards are always there to threaten us, but we try to keep out of their way, and we never see Anthony or Joanne, or if we do see them we do not know it. And there is enough food, even though it is terrible.

We resist, and we do well. We have school every day, and though it is mainly discussion, since we have no paper or pencil (except these, which are almost used up) and only one reader, this book, the children enjoy it very much and it is good. As soon as Gregory has recovered completely, and he is already a lot better than he was, everything will be fine. Raymond is still surviving here after so many years, and we will be too.

And that is all I have to say about us. So the story of us is ending at the same time the book is filled, and no one will find it one day and read it and have to say, "But what happened to Gregory and Kenneth and Lizabeth and Aliysha and Nadia?" Because there was enough room, and they will know. There could be more to write, of how we grow older and all the children develop, but I have written everything that really needs to be said: we are all right, we are just here.

But I have almost forgotten about Miss Love and Raymond, and now there are only a few more lines left, on the very last page of this book. But there is really very little more to tell.

I will write as small as I can:

RAYMOND: Didn't get out? But how could that be? What do you mean?

MISS LOVE: That this is like a nightmare. Oh, I must go and see the children. Oh, Raymond . . .

RAYMOND: But that couldn't be!

MISS LOVE: I do not know, I do not know. Or perhaps we are all———. (I could not hear the last word.)

RAYMOND: But you're being silly! How could that be? You're here with me. Don't you feel me touching you? And now you touch me. Come on.

MISS LOVE: Oh, Raymond.

RAYMOND: See? I felt you touch me. All right?

MISS LOVE: Yes.

RAYMOND: So you see? You're here with me.
MISS LOVE: Touch me.

There was not any more.

by NADIA JOHNSON

THE END